ELEANOR RIGBY

*The chronicles of great love and
fall of the great empire*

ZAMIR OSOROV

PARTRIDGE
A Penguin Random House Company

To order additional copies of this book, contact
Toll Free 800 101 2657 (Singapore)
Toll Free 1 800 81 7340 (Malaysia)
orders.singapore@partridgepublishing.com

www.partridgepublishing.com/singapore

Contents

Preface

This novel is as a keepsake. It comes to us from times irreversable, when the Kyrgyz Republic was still solidly embedded in the USSR and few people dared to dream about an independent future. For most Kyrgyz, contacts with the West were limited to the one-way traffic of Beatles-cassettes brought about by Soviet soldiers serving in Eastern Europe. In those late seventies, early eighties, a period of stability in Soviet history, the events of this story take place. Four students experimenting with telepathy turn upside down their home village when one of them fixes in his dream a date with an english girl. In expectation of her arrival, the students agitate the whole population to tidy up their houses, the streets and in the meantime their morality. Kyrgyz tradition prescribes hospitality, but the isolated village lacks of many elementary conveniences. By depicting the struggle with the bureaucratic authorities which the students have to fight in order to improve the life circumstances, the writer shows the defects of the political system. The novel is a cultural critique, a profound complaint against the mentality of inertness fostered throughout decades of Soviet rule. Though the students are oriented to the West, they love their homeland and keep hoping for a better future.

Now that reality has surpassed all dreams and Kyrgyzstan has become a democratic republic, people ardently try to get rid of the past. Contacts with the West flourish in the form of international organisations which aim to develop a civil society in Central Asia. As a journalist, the author is watching the changes in his country attentively. His novel was an invitation for "the West" to come, but the story doesn't end with it. We can expect a following-up, since these times of transformation are fascinating for all who are interested in the young republics of the former USSR.

The editor,
Kirsten Verpaalen (anthropologist),
1997 year

From author

This novel was been started in 1978 and ended in 1990 year and published on Kyrgyz and Russian in 1992 year. So I counted needful adding some latest commentaries for better understanding how and where and from such reasons and environment originated story and for which kind of results and utterly new reality turned eventually all our world.

Once more this is story about truly love, a deep and strong attraction that have rooted in the hearts two persons, primarily have not any chances for meeting and more even to knowing about each other's existing. She was born in the small town in England, he—in the remotest mountain village of Kyrgyzstan, the part of Central Asia in the 60th years of last millennium. It was time of Cold War, when our world was deeply divided and polarized for two large antagonizing parts—West and East, and between free world and non-free part of it, trapped by the authoritarian comrades, have erected the strong Iron Fence.

It's fairly easy to understand that such epoch was absolutely fatal for love between two honest and kind persons, those lives were divided with such great distances, cultural, political and many others obstacles. From one hand old communists of USSR proceeded creating totally insulated world of "happiness and glory for labor class" and from other hand the West countries gone with own way, protecting themselves from aggressively totalitarian regimes, communistic ideology and addition to all the world faced to perspective of total destruction from suddenly sparking nuclear war.

Nevertheless, the truly love has the greatest transformational, creative and transitional power and we just not imagine what might to happen in our live, time and world if only we able really fell in love from young days as heroes of this story.

For better understanding I conveyed some parts the story with late written poems and references.

So, dear reader, when you submerged to the ground of this novel, written in the epoch of Iron Fence and starting looking around with the eyes of people living in the other side of border, you will also appreciated what happened later through poetic revelations and recollections caused by some great historical, political, and cultural events, belonged to that period.

2014 year

The valley in central part of Kyrgyzstan
in the road between Toktogul and Karakul towns

Part one

*I was ready to go around the whole world
to find somebody . . .*
R. Berns.

I

It all began when we were once, and it seemed to us forever, carried away by telepathy. People from time immemorial believed in the existence of this phenomenon, but untill now science didn't find an answer to its physical nature. Known is only, that at critical moments, moments of intense emotion or shock, people begin to understand each other, even though they may be separated from each other by unsurpassable mountains and forests or immense seas between them.

A case with the sailor, who fallen over a board of a ship on a stormy night, is typical example. Struggling in icy-cold water, the sailor a moment before his death had "passed" tragic information of his desperate situation to his son, who was three thousand kilometres away. The son woke up in the middle of the night crying loudly: "Daddy is drowning! My Daddy is drowning! Help him!" Choking with tears he told his mother, that in his dream he had seen with unusual clarity how his father had fallen over board of a ship into icy cold water. Less then two weeks passed and everything got confirmed as the news about the death of the boy's father reached the fishermen settlement.

Another case which took place in Michael Lomonosov's life is also well-known. The father of Russian great scientist a fisherman from Archangelsk, dying on one of the islands of the White sea "communicated" to his son, who at that time studied in Germany. As a result Lomonosov not only informed about his father's death, but identified as well the place where it all was happening. The news reached him also through the dream. When comrades of his father, the merchants, arrived in Germany and told him that his father had died on one of the islands and that they failed to find his corpse, Lomonosov named the island, where the body was found afterwards.

And lastly a quite "ordinary" example, of a girl, working at a machine tool at the plant. Suddenly and apparently without any reason she felt an intense depression and hopeless despair. Nothing similarly had ever happened to her. Suffering from an awful headache she asked for leave and came home, where she found out that her mother had died of a sudden heart attack.

We can cited endlessly such convincing evidence of the reality of this mysterious. But there's always a tragic and gloomy veil has stretched out upon everything concerning with telepathy. That phenomenon takes place only in such heartbreaking and exceptional cases, connected with death and destruction. In ordinarily life it doesn't display itself completely, while that no mean that it doesn't exist at all. We are just unaware about its existence.

One day, maybe in a not too distant future, when the riddle of this unique biological phenomena will be properly studied, developed and improved, mankind will take great advantage from such way of communication.

It would be a real revolution in our life. Just imagine what may happen, when all people will find themselves able to understand each other. Any time of day or night you could ring any person up, without any cables, wires, commutators, receivers, without telegraphists and telephone operators. It seems to me only after such achievement we will going to be completely civilised and sensible creatures, when each human being's soul opened to the outer world, all innermost thoughts and feelings have been understandable and accessible to everybody, so that everybody must be urge to get rid from all his not so good, maybe evil thoughts, plans and aspirations. Oh! By the time we would turn into perfect angels, wouldn't we?

Certainly together with benefits we face up with a great number of new problems! For example how to reject undesired calls, and find way to people you need without disturbing others, how to protect yourself from thieves-telepaths, robbers and gangsters? There's nothing surprising about it, as any great discovery might be used both for good and evil. And difficulties would be tremendous, but quite solvable, as publicity would be general and absolute. Supposing, someone doesn't want to talk to you, to listen to your complaints, for example, your chief, just hangs up the receiver and all, and you could nothing to do with them, but right in this moment, when your line and hopes breaks off, a lot of other sensible and kind people around the globe would get in touch with you, who sympathise and understand you, they will not only listen to you, but could give you valuable advice, and could even ring your chief up as well to warn him not to make such obvious breaches henceforth, if such breaches were made or show completely other ways and possibilities.

Do you understand the full and exclusively value of such a call, which you lack so much in your real life? And if it surfaced that it is yours guilty, own quarrelsome nature or your professional inadequacy produced crisis the same contacting people will comfort you, they will find some way out from this conflict situation—and everything will be done without bloodshed. And when the things roll down with such way we ourselves will become much better, and all kinds of filthiness, such as bureaucracy, corruption will come to an end; the deepest and darkest waters, and most secluded corners will be brightly lighted. But if some crazy person tries to do something filthy, hundreds, thousands of courageous telephath-Holmses and telephath-Puarrots will rush at once after the bandit.

Mankind will be like to some extent some gigantic cetacean, able to communicate with each other at a distance of hundreds and thousands kilometres, owing to deep-water channels of communication in the ocean. In past centuries, when steamers, tankers, submarine, boats, aircraft carries and other superpower sea techniques had not been invented yet the quality of such kind of submarine communication was perfect, and cashalots lived in all-planetary tribe, exchanging words with each other even if they were on quite opposite parts of the Earth. Fancy such a giant, singing a song to his brother or perhaps his beloved at a distance of more than 10 thousand kilometres!

Perhaps, even that imbending doomsday can be prevented just in this way—the way of rapid establishment of general communication between all people living on the Earth.

. . . *One fine day it will happen, and the world will spread before our eyes and we'll see it wholly, like the magic crystal, with its limitless spaces, blue oceans, hundreds of countries, and great number of cosy and clean towns and villages, scattered on its continents, and then, perhaps, in one of these towns, among the passers in a street, or perhaps at the opened to a garden window, I will see you, a fine strange girl, living so far from me, and perhaps, right at this moment, when my heart is radiating a particularly powerful impulse of love—right at this moment, you are watching me unable to believe your eyes, just as I do not believe in your existence, though sometimes, I see you on the wings of my dream, in my wondrous dreams, elusive, incomprehensibly sparkling.*

Everybody in this world has one irreplaceable love, bestowed on him by heaven, but just a few out of thousands are lucky to realize their dream, for obstacles dividing persons from each other are immensely great and our life is in fact nothing but a continuous wandering in the darkness. Who of us can say that he is absolutely happy? Even if you happen to meet such a person, he exaggerates, he isn't as much happy as he says, but mainly he wishes he were or perhaps just sympathises with you and doesn't want to crush your dreams.

It goes without saying that telepathy promises to render a great service to us in the future, to strighten everything up. I begin to believe that this is really our last chance, that it is a rescue of our life from extinction, alienation and deafness.

A revolution, brought about by this universal means of communication will be much more global and impressive than assimilating to TV or even general computerisation, as we will not only hear each other, but also see the world with other eyes, experience, feelings, think thoughts of each other—without losing ourselves in this ocean of "live" information at the same time. As we will obtain the most perfect devices of near and remote vision and hearing, we will become a hundred times cleverer. The most valuable things of this world will come into everybody's house and become his imperceptible property.

Kolmar town, France

II

Not having realised all these thrilling perspectives, we nevertheless carried on with telepathy, rendering by that a great service to the development of this world.

Briefly speaking, one day we sat down to experiment. The simplest example was as following: locking ourselves up in the room we sat separate from each other, at some distance. Kerim (my partner and friend) would settle on one part of the sofa, bending over the piece of paper and I on the other part, holding a sheet of paper with some childish drawing on it: like a house, the sun, the moon, stars, something of this kind done slapdash. Sometimes we outlined it with ink for more clear "impression" of it in our eyes retina.

At a certain sign I would start staring at one of this drawings,— while Kerim, trying not to think of anything would start mechanically let his pen rove on the paper, drawing the first flashed his mind, his partner on telepathic contact couldn't peep into drawing. Briefly speaking, I was the "transmitting station", and he was the "receiver". I hypnotised him to draw the drawing which was in front of my eyes. After throwing up our cards and summing up, we would change our roles: I was to receive the signs and my friend was to hypnotise me at a distance.

You must have conducted such experiments with your friends in your teenage years or even perhaps in your early adolescence. Anyway telepathy turns heads of much people, especially at that age, when our perceiptivity is extremely intense, when a young man is almost under a shock of its multi promising mysteries. The results of this experiments mainly caused laugh, no more, it couldn't got other way, however, sometimes we were lucky to hit the mark, more or less precisely and accurately.

I still remember how I sent a scheme of a mushroom to Kerim, and he, you just imagine, drew something like a jackboot. It you turn the boot upside down the drawing resembled a mushroom very much,—the resemblance of separate lines and features were so obvious for us, that we congratulated ourselves by that and doomed ourselves for long incarceration and practice.

There was nothing surprising in the fact, that a mushroom had transformed into a boot. It's hellishly difficult and a hopeless matter to discover what the hell some person keeps in his mind, when often he doesn't know himself what and how many things teems in his mind! And how you ask to draw something if you don't concentrate on it? If you ask a four year child to draw a mushroom he is most likely after a half an hour of hard work to depict something like a boot; so did we, making the first steps in our experiments. Thus our wandering in darkness without a guide began. Although each human being trying his best can reach the most amazing results and develop surprising abilities of his soul, nevertheless, only few people succeed in practice. Sometimes the more pains you take, the less promising the results are, it's like a mirage in a desert—as long you go and go on towards it, the vision moves further and further away, till it disappears completely. You finally give up your hope never to return to that and just here the mirage turns up again, and it comes up to you closer and closer, gives you the most convincing arguments confirming the existence of that highest reality, which at times surpass all improbable and fantastic imagination you have.

In crucial moments of life some channels in concealed depth of your heart, soul and mind can catch near and remote signals possessing super conductivity, and we begin to understand each other in a distance, without words, as a son perceives his parents or a lover perceives his beloved. Sometimes at such time we begin to understand people who are quite strange to us, as they also wedge into our superconductive communication. They let us know that they sincerely sympathise with us and regret for not finding a common language in usual life. At such time even your enemies become some kind of friends to you, for telepathy is first of all a powerful mean of rapprochement of people, and not disconnection, it is revelation, giving birth to revelation, and in the end such an increasing wave of mutual understanding can help ennobling us all.

Unfortunately this all happens only in exceptional cases, only when something extraordinary is going on, mostly connected with a huge loss, risk and so on. Perhaps in all that there is some rational kernel, preserving, suppose, our nerve system from unnecessary and permanent overstrain,—or perhaps we have not yet grown up enough spiritually to obtain telepathy absolutely for using it in everyday life. And maybe people of future, each human being from there will have no idea about such a notion as "common life" as we understand it, their life, each hour of their realm and each minute, will go on such a high level, that invisible telepathic communication will be no less than conventional phenomenon, inherent to them.

But what these concealed channels of communication we would turn into, if we mastered them in some way! The channels would have gotten littered and fouled with every kind of talking rot, with long idle chatting, silly sniggering, with anecdotes from all over the world with solutions of hackneyed problems, satisfaction of lowest desires,—such prospects!—giving an opportunity to everybody to wear himself into another person's confidence, to play the master there as he likes. The nature is three times right concealing its miraculous secrets from us.

So, it's no wonder, that most of our experiments, despite our "sizyphean" toil fell pitifully flat. Long before us people much more experienced and conversant than we were—poets, psychologists, whole research institutes concerned themselves with these problems; the scientists of various countries conducted intercontinental experiments on telepathic communications—and nevertheless, despite some certain brilliant results,—there isn't much clearness in this subject, as there isn't any theory, explaining and uniting all this processes and phenomenons.

The efficiency of our experiments was misery: only one shot among hundred hit the mark, and even this could be explained as just an accident, by the theory of probability and not natural result. These were our very first steps, success should have attended us, as it attends everybody, disregarding capabilities, when he is studying simplest things as preface, alphabet, primitive computers game and so on. Insuperable obstacles in front of people turn up later. But, that time we were not aware of that, and having mastered just few letters we attempt investigate with growing ambitions the furthest and the most promising prognosis and realities, naively supposing to pass alone through the darkness, which had swallowed so many people before us.

I'd like to cite a small success we had—it happened during one of our joint lectures, when my friend and were sitting on back seats of the hall and conducted experiments unnoticed to others. Kerim beginning to get tired of it all, he was less patient in such a situation,—went so angry at heart with my insistence, that he, apparently, trying to cut all off, drew quite a nonsense to his mind, just what came into his head, it was what we were after,—and when I peeped into his notebook, almost exclaimed in surprise! He depicted something resembling a hedgehog, and I displayed him my drawing with depiction of the sun with dense, like hedgehog's needles, rays. It worked! Hurrow! It was such a rarest success that supported the creative fire still glimmering in our hearts every time our interest began falling to zero, to the extent when aversion is born.

The bandwidth signal

The secret signal
has hit our hearts
as a sharp sword.

The secret signal
has obliged
for first rate transmission right,

as an emergency car
flying on the busy streets
breaking the all rules
with switched sound,

as an urgent telegram
crying about death of close one
when you received only solemn and cut words
about tragic lost and wouldn't able to do nothing more.

O yes,
sometimes we are shocked by telepathy
and opened hidden channel
between all livings creatures in the world,
accessible and understandable
without any words
in the tragic instants of our existence.

So in the eve of great disaster
or catastrophe
something unusually happen
in the core of substanses and universe around us.
Men, animals, birds, reptiles
trying survive personally
starting to think and do collectively
have transformed behaviorally as close brothers,
when even cruel predators and theirs preys
run out from flames skin to skin
under strong demand of that bandwidth signal.

And so in the end of Times,
as clearly witnessed holly scriptures
not only all living creatures
on the Earth and deep in Seas
but also the souls of all people
had lived in World from beginning of Time

suddenly to awake in the Day of Judgment
when even objects without souls
around us
like mountains, sun, stars
and heaven itself
will trembled, melted, converted and fell down

under pressure of the almighty signal
with the greatest, broadest and deepest
bandwidth capacity
and transformational power.

III

Then in our circle turned up Bolot, a telepath with natural gifts, a little better then we were, perhaps. It was he, who added fuel to the fire, he was a promising physicist and he built a solid physic basis to our experiments, methods of their registration and interpretation. Before that we tried very hard using mainly maths and philology, as I was a student of the department of mathematics, and Kerim of philology, and each had it his own way. As a matter of fact while I acted handling the theory of probability in order to filter grain of regularity from accidental chances, Kerim got valuable observation from creations of his favourite writers, psychologists, exquisite poets "of all times and all people", citing examples, which he considered in some way or the other were connected with telepathy, even if the author didn't suspect of it himself. I wouldn't waste either my or your time telling where and when we got acquainted with him and what kind of figure he cut. We'd better concentrate our attention on main subject— due to telepathy's mysteries, after all, you will learn of each of us later.

Obscure, unconscious interest in telepathy revealed itself in Bolot when he went to the sixth form: even at that time he had reached surprising success with his classmates. It was a plain childish game "guess it"—one would think of a digital number, and others guess. So as Bolot asserted, most of the guys were almost absolutely accurate in hitting the bull's eye. In general, at that age to figure out some beaming figure against on the black background was much easier, and in fact, those receivers guessed instantly the sign,—just with open eyes, in the noisy class. Everything, surely, would happen during breaks.

As years went by, an interest to the game disappears, and this is connected with deadening of telepathic abilities—"children have a lot of games of this kind, connected not only with thinking but also with guessing of other people's thoughts"—he was right in saying so. More than once we tried to experiment in better conditions than noisy class, and every time all our efforts proved to be failures, connected, as Bolot supposed, first of all with the fact that the power of imagination gets weaker as time passes by. Try to imagine some luminous figure against a dark background for a minute and you might see how difficult the task is; your figure will flash and go out and take quite other forms. In childhood everything is somewhat simpler, thoughts are exchanged naturally and easy.

But nevertheless our incredible efforts sometimes were rewarded with good luck. One day, when we were after hours of unhappily training finishing our headache work, will ready go to one of the cosiest and comfortable chihanas of Osh bazaar, known only to us, where they serve particularly tasty peas, saying nothing of green tea, the sweetest sorts of peach, fig, apple, grape and many-many other things from the whole Central Asia. I had no idea why, but in the very end of the party suddenly the figure "9" flashed with unusual distinctness in my mind. It sparkled a second or two, and Kerim, who sat in a semidarkness of the room cried out "Nine!" absolutely sure of his rightness. From the look of my eyes he made out that he hit the bull's eye. We felt a fresh surge of unusual energy that day having experienced a usual small shock in front of the greatest mysteries of the universe.

On the whole, telepathy plays an important role in our everyday life, no matter how weak and insignificant its waves are, in spite of all our attempts not to notice it. Aren't such cases rare in life, when one and the same thought occurs to several different people, sitting in one lecture-hall. Sometimes there're such situations, when apt at telepathy people sort of strike up a voiceless conversation, even if interlocutors sensible to telepathic emissions are on different parts of hall. "What about going to the cinema, old chap? Right now, during the break, I can't stand it any longer!—"And where we'll go to?"—"To *"Cosmos"*, at least for a day seance—an American thriller is on. We won't manage to get tickets for an evening seance!"—"What if the monitor would tell the dean?—"Don't be scared! I talked about it with monitor. He won't even try it". And when the break comes the guys without saying a word would slip the lectures. Sometimes before you open mouth to suggest to go somewhere, your friend suggests the same. A human life is full of some incidents, but most people consider it naively as accidents, as results of similar way of thinking, of natures and corresponding circumstances, which all together bring to coincidences. But these are not accidents and coincidences, there are regularities of telepathy, of inducing thoughts. Somebody offers you an idea, and it seems to be your own idea. My friends and I would rather read the thoughts of each other this way and would often leave for somewhere out of town right in the middle of our classes for 2 or 3 days, dropping everything on earth. It was too boring to be perfect students all the time. There's some particular charm in it: while the others are bustling taking laboratory papers and exams, you are far-far away, at your granny's, enjoying the virgin beauty of nature, and the rest of the world doesn't exist for you at all. You are quite aware of punishment expecting you on your return, but all these are all trifles, vice versa, that feeling of unconscious fear of consequences just sharpens your perception. An incomparably marvellous sun-set you watch on the first day of your run-away compensates for all. "What a right thing I've done!"—you exclaim, feasting your eyes upon the setting sun as if for the last time. By the way, aptitude for telepathy, for passing and receiving thoughts sharply increases at such minutes.

Just imagine running two-three hundred kilometres away from the institute, and perhaps that very moment when you are aiming at that careless rest—eating of grandmothers boursok or catching a forelle or osman at the riverside—a teacher is looking for your name in the register to sign your absence. On the one hand you feel swell, and on the other you are anxious. Uneasy under the influence of such different emotional impacts, you react to good and evil thoughts a dozen times sharper, and this is just the working field of telepathy. Right at such a difficult moment you get to see one who angried against you saying in soul a various bad words at your address, see an expression on the dean's face and other unpleasant things.

A few days later, on your return to the institute you make sure that your vision was close to truth to the slightest details.

You always balance on the edge of the razor, if you want to be a telepath, clairvoyant or a prophet, with the sword of Damocles over your head with the question "to be or not to be?" and the more difficult and uneasy you feel the wider you observe a mysterious sphere of subconscious. Such a Chinese philosophy is an indisputable law of telepathy. Isn't it the reason why all fortunetellers and prophets were deeply unhappy and unsettled, having to sacrifice their lives to the gift they possess. You can not deceive that gift, can not suffer moderately. Here you must pay in real blood, because telepathy doesn't tolerate even the smallest falsehood or pretence. So, make own choice, my friends, what is better for you; to lead a normal human life, but not have seen an inch longer before your nose, or able to see far around you, but living an unhappy life, irritating your relatives and friend by your feebleness and bad luck. It is absolutely clear, that modern man would prefer the first to the second, but nevertheless the great interest to telepathy overwhelms the rest—because that phenomenon too mysterious, enigmatic and powerful for our future, promising incredible good for mankind.

At that time we were already well informed about a series of scientific researches, brilliantly confirming the possibility of transmitting thoughts at a distance. Quite ordinary people, not a bit of extrasense, tell what is going on in environs of New-York to their colleges-receivers, say, in Switzerland, sitting in arm-chairs in a half-dead state in the still darkness of some house.

And what can you say about a successful telepathic communication between inductor at the bottom of on ocean in a submarine and receiver on the shore—at a distance of hundreds of miles.

These facts prove that water is not an obstacle for telepathic waves. In the days of our youth extrasenses and prophets were not as popular as they are today, but even then we lived in anticipation of an approaching era of community's fixed attention to unusual, extraordinary, at times even supernatural capabilities of a human being. Although we had no opportunity to take part in international experiments on parapsychology, where we would have offered with great pleasure ourselves for the various testing as the guinea-pigs, passing thoughts from one continent to the other, got down to the bottom of an ocean in batiscaf, while the other one of us is climbing Everest, and thus be honoured to get to the Guiness book of Records for establishing a telepathic communication between the highest and the lowest points of Earth. Not having all these opportunities we nevertheless were mastering our experiment stubbornly, being locked up between four walls, rejoicing the smallest success so excitingly as though we were discovering America every time we experienced.

Osh[1] is beyond any doubt the most appropriate town on Earth for conducting intercontinental telepathic experiments, as it couldn't be confused with any other town on the Earth, mainly due to its huge Sulayman-Too[2], rising just above town's lively centre and its ancient bazaar. One glance is enough to estimate not only its perfect focusing and other physical properties but also the fact, that this mountain being a thousand people's object of worship is a peculiar source of powerful telepathic waves by itself.

Frontal view of Sulayman-Too

---

[1]   Osh—second largest city in Kyrgyz Republic and one of the oldest in the region, his story begun 3 thousand years ago. Has miraculous features as ancient market, the Sulayman-Too, a great 4-headed mountain, erected right in the center of Osh. Its name translated from Kyrgyz as "Throne of Solomon"

[2]   Sulayman-Too, the most impressive mountain, from where (climbed on top of it) our hero called to his best beloved—Eleanor Rigby from England. By the way the great emperor of Asia Babur loved this mountain more than his empire and sent to Suleman-Too his verses from India (Delhi) where he founded the new capital of his great Kingdom. This mountain included in UNESCO's World Heritage List

IV

One of the most thrilling experiences was the next for us. Certain people are known to be more sensitive to various kinds of psychological impacts, so there's always present a particular sort of human whom you can govern as you like and there are also find such sort of people, who are able to govern others. If a strong person happens to meet a weak one and begins experimenting, you can observe the most surprising things. A sensitive person can be induced to any thought, to do whatever you want him to do. He could be tuned for example to come at mesmerizer's home on certain date and at certain time. For performing and imprinting such task experimentator strains all his will and attention. He figures out the patient coming to his place at an appointed time or performing some other errand, given mentally, at a distance.

And really, after some days or perhaps a week or a month but right at the appointed time a patient performs what he was commanded not aware about it himself. For example, he comes to experimentator's-psyhologists. When a psychologist asks him of the purpose of his visit, what he wants of him, the other usually has no idea of it himself.

He shrugs his shoulders, apologises for his visit and utters that he just wanted to see him, that he does not know how everything had happened,—and the like. It is not difficult to imagine what prospects theory and practice promise, when studied in detail. Without any telephone call you'll be able to call anybody you need, and he will turn up in front of you not conscious of it himself. Certainly, it will work only in that case, when the patient isn't warned of his being under mesmerism. In this attitude telepathy is looking as something like hypnosis at distance. But what is hypnotist in comparison with telepath? The first seems to be selfconfident and roughness personified,—what is good in scaring to death some simple-minded fellow or some fragile plain girl, inducing them to jump, to run right on the stage and perform many other silly things. Though, sometimes it is impressive to watch a man in hypnotic state becoming physically stronger than he is in reality. In such a state he is able to lift even a wardrobe together with the hypnotist himself. As for a telepath, his nature and behaviourism look quite different. It would never occur to him to urge his patient to lift a wardrobe. If a real hypnotist is a god with strong short arms, then a telepath seems to be a divine perfection, calling for the dearest and inmost what a human being has, where to achieve wonder all you need is a dialogue, mutual consent of two hearts, their power; while for a success of a hypnotist just a suppressible and easily intimidated fellow is enough. Hypnosis is nothing else, than triumph of psychopower by its essence, whereas telepathy is triumph of love, bursting through immense spaces into limitlessness.

Now, my dear friends, we could congratulate each other on the main and the most important discovery of our narration, with possibility, due to telepathy, to programmize a date with the person you need. And if you manage to master the secrets of telepathy and hypnosis you could also make a person to fall in love with you. Why not? From the theoretical point of view there's nothing against it, as love is one of the most imposed feelings. I remember when we were on the first year of study some hypnotist-smart-dealer gathered us in the hall, having rushed us three roubles, by the way, and said to the audience: "If I want, all the most beautiful girls sitting here will fall in love with me. If you do not believe, I ask beautiful girls to come up to the stage". Everybody in the hall was scared to death, as most of the guys had come there with their girl-friends, and who would want to lose their friends, and who would want to lose their love? What if some incident would have happened, as our girls were very impressive and our guys were more jealous than all European fellows, though not to such an extent as in most typical Muslim countries of the Orient. One way or the other, things settled fortunately and the audience sighed with relief: the girls of Osh were very shy—who of them would dare to go up to the stage as the most beautiful girl? Then the men had their word, displaying oriental diplomacy to be on the safe side: "we believe you, don't do that, for God's sake!" And hypnotist took pity over them, he didn't make our girls fall in love with him. Perhaps, all that was just a trick, but if you'd better keep off such people. Surely, one may both lift a wardrobe and make an acrobatic feat, and as for a peculiarly sensitive person—they would almost fly over the hall, just give them right command—these all are trifles. And what if a person dear to you, who's cherished warm feelings for you just an hour before would all of a sudden change his mind? A mysterious hypnotist just makes some amendments in your consciousness and it turns out that you've already lost your friend or beloved. No, these are not the things to trifle with. It's better to try an art of hypnosis and telepathy by yourself, not to be afraid of anything and anybody. In this regard the future society will be one of only telepaths, extrasenses and hypnotists, where for that reason nobody could govern the other against his will. Hypnotists, if you have noticed, usually appear before physically and spiritually feeble audiences: students, surviving in theirs learning years of scholarships, the workers of research institutes and project organisations consisting mainly of impressive women; employees of state enterprises aren't satisfied with their life and social position. I've never heard, however, that hypnotist visits chabans[3], one and all are fond of ulak, er sayish, kurosh[4] and other strong physically national games.

They could surely lift a wardrobe or something even heavier to humour a guest, in the mark of politeness—in this case mesmerism is out of the question. They are not the right material for that phenomenon. Quite impenetrable for gipnotic influence, though kind and pliant as human.

But let's leave them all with their sheeps, now the only question of interest for us is: how to learn to manage another person, to make him do something by means of mental impact. If psychologists succeeded in that, why not try it on our average level? Temptation of distant governing's possibilities are great for young people hardly older than eighteen.

---

[3]   chaban—shepherd

[4]   ulak, er sayish, cyrosh—kyrgyz national games, demands braveness and strong physical conditions

Do you remember the invisible man of Herbert Wells? The person, having become invisible is a king among people, he is as powerful and invincible as one who can see among blind men. Something like that described in the novel could perform some genious telepaths, like an experienced chess-player, able to direct others, their thought and feelings distantly, playing all multiple combinations. Such a clear hearing man will be a king among us deaf and blind in general.

But at that time our thoughts were far from possibilities of world's conquer and other awful plans. In the focus of our telepathic impact was something different, namely attention of beautiful girls, especially those, who were for each of us from the rank of inaccessible. What pains we did take in an effort to catch them in our nets. How would we treat them, how would we beg (mentally, of course) to come to dates, how could we mesmerise them, insist on the necessity of coming to us. We used to figure out how everything would happen,—until we began to believe in the inevitability of everything, that our signals had reached the addressees and we were just to wait for results. But they not came to us. You must have tried such experiments in adolescence yourself, if you had been interested in telepathy or had been madly in love with somebody. Now all of those failures seem to have been quite grounded, as we experimented everything in a wrong way from the very beginning, choosing as a material, as an impact's object the most unmanageable, unyielding—as is there anything more unyielding than a beautiful girl, having a high opinion of herself and who doesn't know you at all and whom you try to induce not more nor less than love from first sight and happily family life forever from first sight?

The antidarwinizm of love

Learn from primarily nature.
Eagle do not plunge
for the non-ordinary deer,
cheetah do not risk
hunting for recordsman spring-back,
and celestial falcon
chooses among pigeons
the weakest one
for steep attacking,
and wolf never run
after strong mountain sheep.

Only mister poet
has never learned at all
the basic principes
of economy of force, energy and possibilities,
he preferred ever fours-majors
trying to find, reach, catch and capture
the most fastest
unreachable
unexplainable
unreal and desirable
beauties, marvels and mists
emerging in nature.

No wonder that such anti-Darvinizm
produced so much failures.

I remember Kerim trying an experiment like that, having got acquainted with an extremely pretty girl, who made quite a strong impression on him, him who never allowed himself to be up in the clouds, preferring to see things as they were. But then, something happened to him, he downright lost his head, falling into a telepathic trance,—just imagine, him being in a halfdead state, whispering, that that girl was bound to come to date with him, the next day, at 3 o'clock, to the central station, she couldn't help coming, she would be there waiting for his further commands. Do you see, what I am talking about? He, Kerim, appointed a rendezvous to a girl, whom he didn't know at all: neither her address, nor relatives, nor occupation. So, he called telepathy for help, and was already going to be he husband. And the girl didn't know him at all. They just had exchanged a couple of words, or perhaps, they hadn't. Kerim, as a rule, never missed any chance of that kind,—a girl would just give him a look, and he was sure to start a conversation with her, at least. However, after a two-hour seance of "love meditations" my friend clearly imagined how a strange girl would wait for him next day, at the station, at three o'clock. He took that into his head, believed heart and soul that everything would happen this way, right so and couldn't be different.

We couldn't but believe him, so convinced was he of his adventure's success, and the next day all of us went to the station at the appointed time.

And fancy, that girl turned up at the station exactly at three o'clock, but . . .

She was accompanied by her boy-friend,—and judging by everything she was not going to change him for Kerim, she paid not even slightest heed on the latter.

She was in a high spirit, she was talking to him lively, laughing at something, snuggling up to him, displaying by that a commendable courage, which was unfamiliar for our southern girls. As for the fellow, he was not up to the mark, neither fish, nor flesh. Kerim was even much better, but the girl had chosen him, nothing could be done about it.

Consoling Kerim, we sadly followed them with our eyes. They obviously were leaving for Toleyken[5] anyway, they headed for that direction. The game seemed to be over, but something impossible

---

[5]   Toleyken—small town-satellite on the west of Osh

happened. It worked! the meeting went through, we had a chance from one out of million, but nevertheless, it was an accident, having nothing to do with telepathy. We would experiment a lot in such exercises, but nobody succeeded, despite all our attempts to call girls, to appeal and to lure to them, despite all hopes and illusions we amused ourselves, they wouldn't come and nothing made with it.

And now, when I go through what happened to Kerim again, it seems to me that his experiment succeeded but with no ordinarily way. The meeting was not accidental—it is most likely that spontaneous telepathic contact took place in the very beginning of our experiment, when he appointed a date: "tomorrow, at 3 p.m., at the station". And what was after, during two hours, when he whispered incantation to himself was *post factum*, wasted time, for it was not he, who was a receiver or inductor, but the girl must have imposed on him by power of the charm, that next day, at three o'clock she would be at the station, not suspecting of that herself, of course. In short, Kerim had obviously read her thoughts. He might be pleased with that as an investigator of telepathy, while we hadn't aghast of a chance for success. The girls we dealt with and date with would usually call at us at the wrong time and they were not the kind we longed for, it was, as if telepathy were mocking us and confusing us deliberately: when we began believing in it, it seemed to do everything to dissuade us, and the other way round: when we were already ready to give it up as a lost job to cease puzzling over its secrets any longer, it would all of a sudden lighten up violently, inspiring us against our will.

Only later on we understood, what it was not will, energy and persistence, that was required there. Here all you need is a kind of desperate talent. This way can overcome not the person merely proceding along it, but the one, who is not afraid of running a risk and who can manage to keep the balance all the way long like a rope-walker. Such abilities and inclinations neither Bolot had, nor Kerim and I, one was more, the other was less risky, the third was more assiduous than others, but to have all these qualities taken together and a great talent on top of all was rather inaccessible for us, and it was natural, that we began getting tired of our secret hobby, inspite of its attractiveness and future. It was quite natural. Could we fool around all our lives long? No doubt, transmission of thoughts at distance is thrilling by its essence, but what is the use of cowering under a burden beyond your strength, when you lack talent.

Yes, we began forgetting telepathy, as we forgot growing older many other things from the paradisiacal flower-garden of aspirations and hopes every human being has in his youth and which fails to come true. We would have probably never come back to that subject, would have become more composed and sensitive and have learned to see and comprehend more prosaic, common than telepathy things, which do not require for its cognition special abilities except industry, but on which much depends in your life—everything was coming up to it, to decisive and basic prose of being, and soon we would have ceased even to recall the phenomenon of telepathy (and if we would happen to recall, it would be only on practical purposes, when displaying our outlook) if it hadn't been for Jolchuby.

V

Who was he, in fact? What kind of a person was he? Nothing special, at first sight. A typical fellow, fresh from the country, a broad-shouldered and big-boned person with an excellent shepherd constitution and with somewhat rough features: rather massive lips, nose, little bulging greenish eyes, curly, rather long, shoulder-length light hair. In short, he was of that sort of Kyrgyz, whom we call sari (ginger),—they are easily recognised by a natural bleach light colour of their skin, by light, not always red, hair and by their eyes of the same indefinite colour. You must have already thought that he had repellent appearance, because of my inability to paint him. But it was not so. He was roughly built, but his roughness was harmonic, as if the creator, having conceived to shape a perfect Kyrghyz Apollo but for some reason gave up his job at the last stage of his work, when last traits were left to be worked out: eyebrows to be lined more thoroughly, nose to be ground and other fine points to be completed, this is how Jolchuby appeared. Harmonically and imperfect, fine and plain, rather rough by appearance, but fine inside. It seemed as God apparently had become Kyrgyz himself, in his creation, not putting a finish to his work, or he might have decided, that Jolchuby is rewarded enough as it is. He was the most talented person I had ever met. We estimated him from the first day of our acquaintance, I can say even before that, when we contemplated him in the corridors of the Institute during breaks. Notwithstanding his Martian-shepherd looks, he was very gentle and correct with everybody—these all with his bulging eyes, taken together gave you a wrong impression that he was as shy as a hare. But actually he was as courageous as a tiger, and as strong as an elephant, he was not afraid of anybody, except perhaps of himself. Such a great and strong person must be too cautious among such pygmies as we were.

Before getting acquainted with him we all thought that we must be worth of something, but he turned up—and everything got cleared up. The strangest and the most awful was the fact, that Jolchuby seemed to be good absolutely at everything. It is true, if you are given a talent from Heaven, then you are gifted in full measure. He had shown his worth in natural precise sciences more than in any other field, especially, in mathematics. There wasn't anyone as smart as he was, not only among the students of our Institute, but, perhaps, even among teachers. He had been admitted to the Institute without examinations, as a winner of the republican Olympiad. Due to his ability to get to the point in each subject, he quickly won the confidence of the most intelligent teachers of other subjects,—of physics, chemistry, history, philosophy, literature, political economy, biology. Everybody believed that he would make an excellent mathematician, biologist, economist, specialist in literature; every teacher wanted him to become his disciple. Jolchuby would usually give them hope—if they believed in him, why not justify their confidence? He wanted to please everybody, and surely he succeeded in that, but his abilities and interests went far beyond the limits of University education. Here I do not even mention his success in physical training. It was our first year course of study when Jolchuby had almost become a master degree of sport, having thrown in a fight an experienced wrestler, a champion of our Institute. I do not mention his talent for writing poems, which, like everything in him were striking in by their originality, that he had a good ear for music, as we consider all these as trifles. One of his abilities we ought to speak about particular: he proved to be gifted in telepathy. In the beginning neither we, nor he had suspected of its existence, he was just a mathematician, outstanding personality for us. It was Kerim, who led him into our circle, they knew each other well enough from the first course, when we were on agricultural works. Besides, they were from the same district, and Kerim knew the village, where Jolchuby was born and brought up, though they hadn't met before going to the Institute. They seemed to get to know each other on a cotton plantation. Some elder student was spoiling for a fight deceived by the gentleness of his manners and bulging eyes, taking this traits as sign of weakness. Jolchuby had been take aback at first, he decided not to mix up with that all. But Kerim couldn't stand it, Kera, whom we called a pugnacious fellow, had come up to him and hit him on the head of that bully, the latter had retreated, but returned, with his friends of course. There interceded Jolchuby, he didn't fight with him, he merely took up the strongest of them in the air by the collar for at least a meter from the ground and that was all. For if Jolchuby would have lifted his fist even on the agricultural works, he would have been kicked out, teachers discerned him properly only with the beginning of classes, when they understood what a unique person had come to the Institute.

As for telepathy, he had learned about it first in our circle, and we are proud of that. One day we were at Bolot's, listening to music, when our conversation turned on telepathy, almost forgotten thing, on how we were engaged in it the whole year. I remember Jolchuby became so excited, he listened to us carefully, then asked details and in the end he asked for a list of literature we had used in our study of the phenomenon. In a short time he left us all behind, with all our sum of knowledge on a given subject, he also had read works on biology, psychology, parapsychology, phenomenology, psychokinesis, telekinesis—which we hadn't even dreamed of, and even in books accessible to us he understood much more profound then we did, sometimes even more profound then the author himself. That was where his universal abilities proved useful.

He would approach the incomprehensible and undiscovered phenomenon from all sides, considering the finest details. But even he proved to be a failure in the same experiments on thought's transmission like we did. The failure didn't dampen his ardour, as it had happened with us. He merely shrank into himself and ceased to talk telepathy to us. At times we felt as if he were in another world, even when he was sitting and talking with us, or listening to music— and only later on we evaluated the results of hidden unceasable work of his mind, struck to the bottom of our heart.

The pearly shell of mollusk

On the dark bottom of sea,
under the miles of deep salt water
one creative mollusk
dedicated his life
for searching
the sacred dream
about majestic and precious
pearly sunrises
somewhere far above the sea.
And eventually
this artist filled up
inside wall of his home
with his dreams—
created the most beautiful
rendition of sunrise.
The eternal beauty, my dear,
receded herself to him
and hosted in his nice chamber
in the darkest bottom of sea.

VI

This happened in 1984, three years after we had graduated from the Institute. You are probably shocked by the exact mention of a date, usually only two of the first figures are cited, but the matter is that I will be even more exact further, accurately fixing the month, week and day the wonder witnessed. We met at the same place, at Bolot's house, where Jolchuby first learned about telepathy—at the foot of grand Suleyman-mountain. By that time we had already seen much of life, working in different parts or the country. So we seldom had opportunities to see each other, just once or twice a year. By the way, that day it was for the first time we gathered together in full, the four of us after our graduation. It was a particular pleasant get-together made possible only owing to the initiative of the host of "the house at the mountain foot", who sent each of us the telegrams, read "We three (our names, except the name of whom the telegram was addressed) are waiting for you, the fourth. "That simple and naive plan succeeded— and we, at last, gathered in Osh, three years after graduation from the Institute. It became a decisive meeting, made 1984 as important for us, as 1961 was for 4 fellows from Liverpool, who found each other finally to change the world.

That meeting was dear for us yet for another reason, as with Bolot's house, with his room our recollections of student years were connected. Along the wall of the room stretched shelves, from floor to ceiling, filled with books. There were about three thousand books, accurately placed on the shelves. To the left of the room there was a sofa, behind it was a small desk, a couple of armchairs, a chair; opposite the door was a window, looking out to Suliyman-mountain. The tape recorder stood on the window-sill.

But in the house there were other amusements besides music and books. Bolot's mother would always regale us with something delicious, sympathising with us as students. She was a simple woman, but you'd be mistaken, if you thought, for example, that she knew little about literature: she was an intellectual, knew a thing or two about different sides of life, had a subtle perception of poetry and music, of which we made sure more than once.

It's always pleasant to meet an intelligent personality, and outstanding in all respects, but when this person remains kind and plain at the same time, you're almost happy and begin believing in a bright future, where everything would be pure, perfect and simple, where New-York would become as native and hearty as your own village, which in its turn would turn into the most perfect town in the world not only in your dreams.

This house helped keeping our dearest recollections. Especially if we took into account that all of us during students years had lived, cooped up together in hostels, where we would very often underfeed, freeze, languish with heat during summer—time, suffer from disorder, caused both by our inability to put order, to overcome our craving for all kinds of excesses, like weakness for alcoholic drinks. When right after the getting of scholarships many students would arrange such a bacchanal that after they would live only on water and bread the whole month. It is necessary for a person to have comfort to be well, such a comfort as in this home, where everything is provided for normal life. A fine library, well working heating, a general high intellectual level of the family, fine human qualities of the mother, order and cosiness in the house, view of Sulaiman-mountain from the window of the room where we were sitting and recollecting the past. Bolot's mother, and the joy with which she met us—these and many other things, merging together, created domestic surroundings. So many hospitable families lack this sound harmony. Everybody lack this or that, some of them are ready to cram you over with delicatessen, but quite forget about spiritual nourishment as you could be fulled up not only with excellent food, but you also need good intellectual conversation, others on the contrary have their parties well thought out from the intellectual and spiritual points of view, but pay no attention to material point, someone lack light others lack warmth, the third have these all in plenty, but inspite of his cordiality you can't be quite yourself.

But that evening we didn't feel like discussing such everyday dull things as questions on etiquette and piety of hospitality. Who were we to judge others? Let clever people think of that and when the appropriate decision is taken, objectives and subjective for alteration come ripe, then we'd try not to let them down, relying on common sense. We did not expect great things from life, exploit and valour are not for us, we just wanted to be happy and be satisfied with life. We wanted to promote everything that would advance society even for a step to summits of civilisation and culture.

But can you imagine, even at such a small thing we hadn't allowed ourselves, the life put enormously heavy burden as if in our country there weren't any other men and its destiny depended completely on us four.

Thus everything began that day, when we were sitting, together in Bolot's room, relaxed, forgetting for a little time any problems, listening to old records of "Beatles", so even such a trifle in another minute breaked for us.

Yes, it was he, our unpredictable Martian. He was sitting on the sofa, with the head leaned back, his eyes closed. And then all of a sudden abruptly he moved forward, abruptly turned his face to us and stared at us with his green eyes as a drunk had recalled something very important, of which he immediately lost his intoxication.

VII

—What happened?—Bolot was first to react on his sudden change.

—You want to make us all stammer?—murmured Kerim,—another jerk like that would turn the house upside down.

—Do you know? But you won't believe me,—his voice fall,—well . . . I've mastered telepathy! I've got its point, I carried out the phenomenon in practice,—he leaned back on the sofa again, and closed his eyes.

—Is that all?—we signt with relief. Bolot gave an ironical smile, Kerim hopelessly waved his hand, because we had the most experienced, arch telepaths. At first I thought that Jolchuby conceived to play a trick, but the expression on his face was too serious, I read a hidden fear and uncertainty in his eyes.

—Well, let us listen to him. You're out of mind, I see. Johnson, stop blinking and tell us everything as it is.

—Swear you keep a secret?

—Sure, maybe you don't believe us?—answered Kerim.— Though, we can swear, if you don't believe.

—I've established a contact with one person. No, no, I'm not kidding,—he stopped Kerim by the wave of his hand, who was going to put in a word.—This is very serious, I've established a contact with a person.

—Hm!

—I swear, if you think I lie. I've got in touch with the girl. She lives far from there.

—Why are you dawdling? Who is she? From where? Why? Don't you see it is ridiculous to watch such a giant like you turn into a mumbler?

—She lives far from here. I didn't tell anyone about her, but now I have to do it. It is no good to hide it any longer. One should run a risk, undertake something.

—All right, we'll help you.

—You know, we are likely to get married in nearest future, and I must warn my parents.

—Ah. Now it is clear. You should have said that from the very beginning. But what it has to do with telepathy? Marriage is a earthly thing, isn't it?

—The matter is, Sull (they often call me so, though my full name is Sultan), that I found my love thanks to telepathy,—and then he turned to Bolot and asked:

—Say me, please, you've been brought up in town, what in your opinion Russian girl is like when she becomes a wife? Is it true, that they are too exigent? That she almost ignores her husband's relatives. I've heard much negative opinions about them, I even know examples, when a Kyrghyz husband separated complete from our mather and father, by the own freely will, preferring living with love as a marionet. Are European women really so despotic, fretful and wilful? That they can't do without gaining the hand over their Asian husbands? Agreeing to a free marriage-contract only on such terms? Surely our men are all lumps, that they could allow a woman more than she is allowed by nature?

—Well, It depends on the woman you happen to meet,—smiled Bolot.—But I think, that women have appreciated first of all by their qualities, and only then by their nationalities.

—You are quite right,—confirmed Kerim.—Even a Kyrghyz wife may turn out to be such a serpent, that would take not your parents, but even yourself into her hands. You can do nothing about it—an era of matriarchy is approaching. Why, we have a very interesting theme to discuss, as I see. Are you going to marry a Russian girl, Jolchuby?

—No, it's not . . . so simple,—raising his hand Jolchuby, asked for patience, then cleared his throat and began:

—The most difficult thing in the world is to perceive yourself. Who he get deeper his own world, his own universe then succeeds more in his life. We know nothing of this Universe, and as one clever scientist noticed, we don't even know that we know nothing. And the most strange thing is that you have to search that immense world, whose master is you.

You have to go through dense jungles all alone, which are full with all kinds of dangers, waiting for you at your every step, certainly, it is in that case when you really are set to master this thickets, when you go further and further through brushwood and not stick to some safe place, ploughed and improved before you. What I have found there was just liquid spring, full of cold water, but even that is not little, and soon you'll understood that. Certainly, there were many other springs and lakes, hidden away, some magic worlds but I discovered only that spring, and when I drew water palmful, to quench my thirst I saw in water, as in mirror, my destiny. At first I had no idea how difficult it would be, how incredibly difficult; at that time I wasn't aware of obstacles, waiting for me on my way to my spring, otherwise I would have most probably lost courage to run a risk.

VIII

View of Kyzyl-Suu[6] valley where nested one of the remotest mountain village in Kyrgyzstan with the same name

Everything had begun from the queer and mysterious dreams, which would call on me from time to time, once or twice a year,

---

[6]   In the 1960-years of last century in the small mountain village Kyzyl-Suu of Kyrgyzstan (Central Asian part of USSR) was born kyrgyz child Jolchuby. His father was shepherd and his family poor but boy was clever and extraordinary and his country was majestic. He liked to see far Blue Mountain and sing a song climbing up to green hills in spring. He was studied at local school and after it arrived to south capital of Kyrgyzstan—Osh, where learning in University and firstly heard about music of Beatles (it was a "Girl's" interpretation by local music band) and loved it. But it was not just a love rock music. Beatles awaken in the soul of Jolchuby deep and primarily existed dreams and senses. He feels that overwelming by something maybe even bigger than out planet.

44

almost from the cradle, making the deepest impressions me, shocking me so soundly, that I would live under their impression for months.

Why do some dreams deceive and mock us, turning everything over, whereas other dreams present us truth so fully, that to realise, to conceive it turns out to be beyond our power. What is the structure of a dream, its ground, aim and predestination?

Where does it come from and where does it leads to? Without any doubt, that dream was some kind of reflection of the reality in which we live. In our dream we see, as a rule, the fragments of this reality, as the streets of the town you live, familiar to us or seen just once. Very often the reality presented in distorted, primitive and confused form, in such dreams the geometry of space, feelings and perceptions took sheer non-Evklid character. Nevertheless we orientated ourselves easily in this confusion, knowing the sources, the ground, the events and impressions of that or this vision. It was all plain and understandable but one question wouldn't give me any rest, suggesting variants of its interpretation. "If the dream is a distorted reflection of what we see or have seen, hear or have heard even once in life, then why in other dreams we see people unfamiliar to us, with whom we have never met, we see lands, where we've never been before, experience feelings, unknown before—is it a free fantasy of an artists dream? What is artist's dream, drawing something non existing or are they the fragments of reality, which dreams have reflected in some mysterious way in night travelling all over the world? Perhaps ancient Greeks were right when they asserted, that dream lived its own life. What if dreams, like people, are able to exchange information, to mix up? If so, how to tell these extraordinary dreams from ordinary dreams?

I spent much strength looking for answers to those questions, much is unclear for me even now, but in one case among thousands, or even millions, I managed to hit the bull's eye. I made a miracle, working my way to a hidden spring through the forest of my Subconscious, full of wild monsters and predatory animals, swarming with apparitions and werewolves. I realised, that what had been calling me since childhood existed in reality, that those wonderful lands and people, whom I saw there were more than just a dream.

It is the phenomenon of telepathy, confusing thoughts and feelings of different people, making them clairvoyant to each other. A man in telepathic dream not only see the other, but he gets inside of him, installs himself there, becomes part of him, begins to see the world with his eyes, the latter experiences the same, but in opposite direction. **That is what we call a dream-contact, a dream of mutual enlightenment.** The most difficult part is to learn to tell such a dream, without falling for other temptations of conscious, of imagination—to know how to extract grains of gold, sorting out tons of dross. It was incredibly difficult, but just there I used all my abilities of thorough analysis and scrupulous systematisation of my observations and results of experiments which I performed unceasingly—consciously and subconsciously, in dream and in walking hours when I got utterly absorbed in abyss of mind, though it sounds vague. On the whole, it is not possible to tell the technical points even perfunctorily, I'd better give you my thick diaries and if you get interested, and you can not only get the details, but as well try to do what took me years. However this is an obscure and not very pleasant matter, not that I am talking you out of that, but I am merely afraid, that you would be deeply disappointed in the end and would subconsciously blame me,—Jolchuby, breaking off his talk, hung his head and mechanically pressed his head with his palms, as if his head was cracking from pain. But his head was more probably aching of surplus of thoughts and feelings, attacking him from all sides, and he hardly managed to put some order in this flow, despite his unusual abilities to systematisation.

—So, the essence of the matter is,—rose his head again Jolchuby,—that when two compatible or kindred nature persons think and dream of the same way,—roughly speaking, not going into details,—that at certain moments the pulsation's of their thoughts and feelings may coincide, and they begin feeling each their perceiving each other. That is telepathy. If at that moment happen not only some intersection of thought but also their coincidence by the phase takes place, then telepathic communication is performed, which will give way to violent shock, of which I've already told. If it's going on in a dream (at least for one of communicating parts),—then you have a telepathic dream, if in a walking state—then a person gets caught in unconscious enlightenment, he feels a fresh surge of energy, he is in such a state, when he feels like singing. It is evident, the world around you answers your feeling; kind thoughts call kind thoughts, accumulate in one place, while ill thoughts are able to attract and multiply ill thoughts and can bring finally to death. This is well-known to extrasenses. The matter is, I suppose, in resonance of good and evil in us and around us. If the resonance of the first overwhelms—we feel good, if it overwhelms to a greater extent—we are the happiest people in the world; but when evil overwhelms good—the evil around us "answers" you, increases your private evil, producing even more evil, plunging into dangerous deeps of endlessness. That is why fairly strong person can make his surrounding people happy, to some extent, thus charging them by light and energies, while at the same time gloomy environment may kill any light in the nature of people. But they are just general mankind's problems to be solved by extrasenses, as for me, getting mixed up accidentally with that, I managed to get out of it, and now my task is a totally different one. I must get ready to a new life. That is all, I think.

How Pity

**How pity
that our people
will not to live
in a future,
make an instant leap
for one or two centures ahead,
when the most part of world
could transform so beatifully
as a temporal Switzerland,
that opened us from Rainfelden,
a little town near Basel,
faire-tale and outlook
for the eternal dream of Mankind.**

The view of Rainfelden, a little town in Switzerland

IX

—What does it mean—a new life?—we didn't quite understand, while his pause was endured.

—I . . . I don't know . . . how to say it. Everything seems to be all right. All difficulties are left behind, the distressing world of uncertainly doesn't oppress me any more, but at the same time, everything is just beginning,—it was funny to watch Jolchuby changing his scientifically vocabulary into childish uncertain babble until he blushed again ashamed of his uncertainty, and uttered abruptly:

—Well . . . My beloved will come to me after four months,

—You mean your bride? Really? You should have said this from the start. If it's got so—you are lucky to have such a friend like Kerim.

—Tell us the truth, you've obscured it all because you wanted us to help you to steal a girl for you, haven't you? If it's so don't worry, old chap. No one is as good at it as I am. No, matter who your girl is, where she is from, no matter how her parents guard her, Kerim will come and steal her[7].

—No, it's something pretty oddly. She is an entirely different girl. Not ours, you see?

—What do you mean when you say she is not ours. We have nothing that doesn't belong to us. If she is Russian, it means she isn't ours? Forget it! We are all equal in our country. So will be kind—and steal everything what you see around yourself. Or perhaps you meant something different. Or is she from another planet? Is she a mermaid with a fish tail? Why do you talk about her this way?

—Tell us the truth, Johnson, say that she is Russian, that you got acquainted with her during the trip you wrote me of?—decided I to display my perspicacity.

—Ha! You are quite like Sherlock Holmes,—Kerim said caustically.

—It is clear as it is, after all has been said. Say, did some blue-eyed beauty, some slim birch put a spell upon you? And you, you are like a crooked brunch of archa[8] stuck to a cliff, growing high in mountains.

Jolchubai didn't say word, he didn't even grin, he seemed to be quite estranged from everything.

—Then who is she, damn? Look, what a pretty girl is passing down here,—Kerim opened the window wider, turning his back to us.

—Wait a little,—came to himself Jolchuby,—Well, she . . . she lives far from here . . . , hm . . . in a small English town called Darlstown. This is my innermost secret.

—Say it! You want us to make believe you. Play a trick again? Maybe I run after the girl before she disappears? Eh,—he said regretfully.

—I am not kidding, she really lives in England,—went on Jolchuby without lifting his head or changing the expression on his face.

—Oh! It could be told by your face. We do not know how to get to Andijahn, and you are talking about of England. What is the

---

7   In Muslim countries stealing a girl in order to marry is an ancient custom, often without asking for her consent.

8   Archa—a tree, which grows in mountaineols regions of Kyrgyzstan.

name of your girl? Isn't she Julliette? Then I am Shakespeare, my dear Romeo, my gogle-eyed wonder, excuse the old chap,—Kerim was irrepressible that evening, and by some strange inspiration began to vie with Shakespeare himself, by reciting a poem:

> Be my faithful beloved
> If my first wife allows.
> Assent, my dear Julia
> I won't love you long.
> And then, oh then, if you permit,
> I'll find another one.
> And I will have three wives, you see,
> And all of them will be devoted to me.

The room kept quiet for a moment, absorbing this poetic tirade, and then everybody bursted out with laughter, and so strongly, that all characters from the books, standing in Bolot's library seemed to be laughing with us. And Jolchuby was laughing loudest and most infectious of all.

—Hah-hah-hah-hah! You are a brick! Hah-hah-hah! Here he even got up and coming up to Kerim, clapped on his back.—Ha, my dear Julia. Here you noticed right, if the first wife allows. The rest we could do by ourselves. That is why I am telling you this,—he dropped his voice, wiping away the tears.—And you have already lost your faith in telepathy. That what telepathy is, when you perceive and work over information you get particularly keenly both by your mind and heart. Thank you, buddy, you owe me a great service by your joke. But if seriously, chaps,—Jolchuby's expression on the face became depressed again, the change was quite considerable.—What am I to do now? How to meet my Julia? Where to start?

It became very quiet in the room as before, even restless Nosdrev[9] became all ears. This time it was Kerim to come up to Jolchuby, and looking into his eyes he asked:

---

[9]   Nozdrew—the personag from novel by Gogol "Deads souls", known

—Hey, buddy, what is the use of this crap? You'd better turn to psychiatrist, as well as we should, what do you think?—Kerim looked at us.

—Who knows,—I whispered.

—I've told you the truth, and you have felt that you must admit it,—said Jolchuby.—It is telepathy to be blamed. Can't you understand that? Quit laughing! I've got in touch with a girl, who was born and brought up in England.

—Is it really?

—Yes, indeed.

—Oh, cute!

—Is she beautiful? Or not very much? Oh, I know these English women with their short noses. That's good. You are a brick! That's what you are up! Wonna get a girl from the costs of foggy Albion? I wonder, who will let you? What if some uncle from Scotland-Yard would tell you to get out? What will you do? Surely you'd hit him, wouldn't you. Well . . . I've never heard anything like this. But I guessed there was something wrong with you, especially on the last year of the Institute. Why, I would wonder, Johnson had quit talking about girls. I liked to tune him to this subject in order to enlighten myself. Do you remember, once we had a talk about Japanese women? I still keep your words in my mind: our girls, even when they are very beautiful, lack something, some piquancy, I think. Right words that were, you even explained me, what particular piquancy. And now, I see you turn your attention to quite another object, and now nothing else remains but to feel sorry both for Japanese and Kyrghyz girls—just think of it! Jolchuby rejects them forever, his heart now completely belongs to a blue-eyed beauty from the bank of Thames. You say, it is telepathy to be blame, not you. Well, unbosom yourself, tell us, how it happened. Sorry, I won't interrupt you anymore.

—Please, tell us,—we backed his request, knowing of his strange nature. If he dislikes something he just would leave without saying a word. Thus would have happened this time, if the joke of Kerim had

---

for his noisy nature.

not been so apt. Jolchuby, to our great joy, didn't put his revelations off, but went on, silently demanding earnestness and affection from us.

X

Perfect vision

Perfect knowledge
equals to perfect vision.
We have clearly seen
and observed what happening
in close and far distances
only through sharped eyes and honed mind.

And even more
through precise focusing
we cleaned various details and features
our surrounding reality and background of existing
tending made more harmonies in this world,
through support and create
sharpness and comeliness
around us and far away
in close and great distances,
in space and times.
We are honing our eyes
and world perfectness together
through instantly efforts
and long termed effort and diligence.
So nothing change
if we have wrong knowledge and vision.

"You probably remember that great astronomer of the past, who discovered a star unknown before with the tip of his pen,—owing to thorough mathematical calculations. This unknown star was Pluto, invisible in a night sky with naked eye. So, this astronomer paid attention to splashes of gravitational orbit of other visible planet of solar System, next to Pluto caused by attraction of invisible one, and by these splashes he calculated not only the size and mass of the invisible planet, but also its location on the map of the starlit sky fairly accurately. On the same evening he directed his telescope to this point, and the world knew about the discovery of the sixth, or seventh planet of the solar system.

—The most amazing fact is that there were two astronomers, discovering that planet at the same day. But the first lived and worked in England and the second in France. The whole civilized world excited about the greatness of human mind, its genius, though all calculations now seem elementary,—commented Bolot. Jolchubai, nodding, continued.

—The fact that they made this discovery together doesn't seem accidental for me. I suppose there was something dealt with telepathy, and this case confirms best all that I talked about earlier, namely: if, suppose two persons, in this case two talented astronomers are in search of the solution to one and same problem and in addition have similar natures, souls, ways of thinking, then at certain moments of creative enthusiasm they begin to feel each other, as long distance sportsmen feel each other's breathing, each other's elbow. It is this hidden struggle, hidden contest of intellects and at the same time mutual support, enlightenment and enrichment of each other (of which neither parts is aware) that contribute to the success of an affair. Acting all alone is more difficult. By the way, in the world of sport records are attained only due to keen rivalry, when rivals equal in strength are chosen. Although occasions of telepathy are rare here, except such kinds off sports, as football, where for the success each player's and the speed of thinking of the whole commands is necessary in the first place. I am talking about this, it seems to me that such extraordinary sportsmen as Maradona often act as telepaths, reading thoughts of their partners and rivals. In creative activity the moment of telepathy is even greater, especially in scientific work, where the efficiency depends completely on brain's activity. Surely, I do not assert that scientists literally read each others thoughts, but there is something that let you pose such hypothesis. The fact, that approximately 2/3 of scientific discoveries in the field of mathematics are duplicated, that is they are made not by one, but several scientists simultaneously, independent of each other, asserts the same. Doesn't it seem to you, in minutes of highest creative enlightenment that someone invisible watches you? I experience this very frequently, though there can be various interpretations to it. But let us refer them to the psychologists of the future.

All my life I seem to have been under influence of "gravitational" forces. With the best will of the world I can't tell you everything I've experienced, I'll just dwell on some details for you to have a general idea of my sufferings, that unveiled what is maybe the greatest mystery of my life.

As all country children in our backward and neglected provinces I grew up as a sensitive and dreamy kid, I could dream for hours and even for days, especially in winter time, when snow lay waist high in the village of Kysyl-Suu, and classes in school were suspended and nothing remained but to sit locked up at home.

Well, I was a great dreamer, I was getting ready for performing heroic deeds, in order to be recognized by people of my country as a person with unusual of abilities, one able to fly over the fields in blizzard, who comes to rescue people in calamities, able to master many other skills; to drive the fastest cars, to climb the highest mountains, to travel the whole world over and tell of the countries I've seen to my fellow-villagers some of whom have never visited even the centre of the district. But all these deeds were somewhere in future, and my present was extremely dull and prosaic. I was an ordinary boy, always absent-minded because of my "reveries", whenever I was—at home, at classes, on hills over the mountains, where I used to shepherd; my blank look, my constant submersion into my inner world would very often betray me. Only in the world of my own, the world of fantasies and tales I was completely happy, and the world around me seemed to be of no importance for me. Most people around me were irritated, worried and amused by my behaviour. My school life would have turned into a hell for me, as you know in schools such sort of meek and dreamy creatures were not much respected, but though I was meek, physically I stood head and shoulders above all my classmates and even chaps older than me. So, in this respect I was an exception to the general rule, and could act as I liked and not follow very cruel claims and terms of a teenager's world. At home I would usually find my father's support, who was not quite typical for a person of our province: though being self-taught he collected a decent library, almost the whole classical literature, but at the same time he remained a simple person, though he could have become at least a teacher at school. So my father approved of my aspirations, mainly because I liked to listen to him to recite poems from his thick books, whereas other members of our family got soon bored from that subject. Actually my father considered me to be intelligent, especially at perception of poetry.

But all the same, I would very often, amusing everybody with my awkward actions. Now, when I come to recollect those years that behaviour of mine doesn't seem queer, it was normal to be involved in the field of some gravity but still unconscious of this fact. But at that time I hated myself for my forgetfulness. Very often I would lose myself in reverie during classes, though I tried my best to be on the alert to keep it at a distance I would badly blush every time the question of a teacher reached me through a misty shroud and I just wouldn't know what to say in reply. I would just stand like a dumb. One occasion I will never forget. Well, once I let myself to whirl after some reverie for a flash, when right at that moment the teacher breaking his explanation off asked me to fetch something and pointed to the door. Having understood nothing, I got up from my place, came up to the door and went out to the corridor quite mechanically, and only there I saw, that I had understood nothing and thus got into the silliest situation. Nothing left to be done but peep into the class again after some time and ask the teacher: "Sorry, what did you send me for?"—Imagine my physiognomy when asking. The class burst out in laughter, but the teacher just smiled and articulated his request again: "Fetch the register. It is left on the table in the teacher's room." I was pleased with the tactfulness of the teacher, others would most probably have mocked in presence of my class-mates. In school you take everything oversensitively; not the way you do as an adult.

XI

It was just the outside of the matter, and it may have been not so essential. The most important was happening inside of me. When I was at fifth or sixth form I felt a strong urge to study English. You know, I was good at this subject at the Institute as well, and my English teacher usually passed me, saying something like: "Very good, Jolchuby, I am astonished at your success!" And at the last examination in the end of our fourth year I spoke about 10 minutes on a free topic, after I had done with all her tasks, and she said to me. "In Kyrghyz language there are about forty-fifty English words. I keep puzzling over the way they got there. Perhaps these are some mathematical miracles of accidental coincidences. But since I've been working with you, it seemed to me that there was something different behind it and perhaps, English is in some way kin with Kyrghyz language. I have worked on probation for four years in Oxford and can say with all certainty, that your English prononciation, young man, is so perfect, that even if you make mistakes, your mistakes are like that of a real Englishman. How that comes?"

Certainly, the English teacher was exaggerating deliberately to give me some pleasure at parting, as I was her most industrial student. Even now I regard her words as a joke, as a fine and subtle joke. The matter is that I had a real passion for English. Comprehension of language leads to comprehension of its native speakers, it is as if you by getting inside of a language begin to understand its traditions, its culture.

—The contrary is also correct,—I decided to put in a word on the subject thrilling me for a long time.—Attraction to a nation, to its culture and history causes some great interest to the language, doing progress in learning inevitable. In short, if you like some nation, then you are bound to love its language and will never miss a chance to learn it. If you have no love for the nation then it is doubtful whether you would want to learn it's language.

Jolchuby nodded at me comprehensively, fully agreeing with me. Then he glanced over us three, sitting in front of him in tense expectation (probably he wanted to check whether he bored us and to make sure of the opposite) he went on:

—Actually, I mastered English as well as Russian. My knowledge of a small island state in Western Europe was growing day after day, a year after year, the more I knew of England, the more interested I got. It became for me as intimate and comprehensive as my own Kyrghyzstan—if the first was an island in the outer circle of the Atlantic Ocean, then Kyrghyzstan was a mountain island in its own way among immense deserts and semi deserts of Central Asia, separated from the gigantic mountains of Tibet and Himalayas.

Oh, it was an extremely complicated society, one of the most unique nations of the world, the history of which, as Marx said, was inimitable in its integrity and completeness, it remains an inaccessible model of perfection in its way as Ancient Greece. Voluntarily or not, but everything seemed to attract and fascinate me in this country, was it the music of "The Beatles", or forward of combined team Kigan, or Turner, Chesterton, Byron, Sherlock Holmes, Hardy, Haggard, or suspension motor way, winding like serpentines, or procurators wearing wigs, London's Big Ben, Oxford University, stories by Chaucer, contradictions of the English nature, sonnets by Shakespeare, cricket, a play unknown to us, these and many other things attracted and worried me as, well, not only as things and phenomena, perfect in their own, but as something more . . . I don't know how to say it,—as something intimate and native to me. No, it was not passion of investigator and enthusiast, because there are so many other countries in the world, not less rich and highly developed, and among them there are many countries closer to me genetically and historically.

And one day I asked myself a question: what was the point of my such a strong passion for England? Was I am Englishman, gone astray to Kyrghyzstan a long time ago? No, that was not the case. None of my ancestors had ever seen Englishmen, neither had they seen even a sea shore. In short, they were the Kyrghyz. I was not even a scholar, a specialist of English, or linguist, was not an artist, public figure or even the teacher of English in a secondary school. Surely, England, as one of the most highly developed countries of the world could easily arouse an interest. Especially those people and nations, who are now just on the stage of development, who still have to learn how to make use of their opportunities, as did England and a few other countries. There's nothing strange about it, it had always been so, and it would be so forever. All of us fell in love with England forever after John Lennon and Paul McCartney cherished the whole world with their music,—so simple, so understandable and accessible. But I was not a fan of them and couldn't even stand such people. Do you believe me, when I say that even if Sir McCartney himself with his "Wings" arrived by some miracle in our town, I wouldn't wear myself out to get to his concert. I would try to get tickets, of course, but not more than that. On the whole, "Beatles" has never been a sacred thing for me, but all the same, like a prominent cultural phenomenon it played a certain role in my innerworld, it was some kind of orientation in the set of values of the West; I know that this worldwide quartet of really talented young men said their weighty word in music and proved that a human being could turn over the world without violence and wars. Their music isn't forgotten till now, it seems to me that it is really the greatest rock group of the century. But not more than that. There are hundreds and even thousands of other miracles in England, equal or even surpassing the given phenomenon. But unfortunately our youth as well as the older generation knows nothing about England, except "The Beatles".

But, the matter is not in "The Beatles" and a great number of other miracles, which abound in this wonderful country,—*my interest had appeared much before I knew about it all*, in my school days,—even now, 20 years later nobody in Kysyl-Suu knew about "Beatles", only a few, who discover it like America. Apparently, it was something else, more primordial and profound than this all.

Later on I became acquainted with telepathy, which gave me a powerful incentive to all my dim passions and latent desires. It developed, formulated and grounded much of them—as if I'd obtained the second sight, and a world, unknown to me before, lay open in front of my eyes. By that time the best I had in me got somehow connected with the island in the North Sea, and now, when it flew out from the cage of ignorance, like a bird, parts of the world opened before me—the matters took a swift turn. Though I have a clear mind and phlegmatic nature, my heart, nevertheless, made exceptions for foggy Albion, and till now, once I think about it I got into euphoria, everything connected with that country began appear to me fine and perfect: their women are the most beautiful, the people the most developed and democratic, where from four people one is bound to be crank and eccentric, the land, culture, sport—shortly, the whole of Britain seemed the centre of the Universe, sometimes I found myself to be more Englishman than Kyrgyz, though I tried to conceal that from other's, even friends. And actually, something seemed to be wrong about my passion, so I would think, at least. In fact, what could it all mean? What is England for me, and what am I for England? You could love a girl, lose your head because of her, but you can't possibly love the whole country like a girl. It was nonsense, some sort of addiction, called anglomania. But a single thing remained unknown, what fed this decease, from where this warm wave, dim hope came, which is wind's breathe and leaves' rustle, which sustained me for a long time and sustain me now every time I start thinking of my favourite subject, start perceiving some part of its limitlessness, and perceive myself at the same time, as if inspired by some angel?

An English limerick

There is flourished a country-garden named England,
where various skeletons, monsters and vampires
have kept carefully in cupboards, or chained and locked in frames
of strict rules,
when in our own countries all our demons, witches, gins and gools,
freely walking along our streets,
feeling comfortable in our flats,
in our politic, states offices, private and common lives
and in religious ceremonies and others treats
and traditions.
English no better than Kyrgyz
and no steeper
they are just trained
to hold themselves
and their powers strictly.

In their natures
in the deep corners of their souls
burned the same passions
that outbursted
from our bosom
as protuberances
making many destractions

There is flourished such country as England
well trained to protect themselves and all citizen nerves and gangliers,
from emotions, quarrels and others untied extravagancies,
and with that aims covered by neat parks, gardens and squares
as one wholly sanatorium
grown and build with effort and zeal of many generations,
where now walking and resting in the end of days
very nice and polite misters, gentlemen, misses and ladies.

XII

And then I had this dream, the dream that—as became clear to me—had been following me ever since childhood, remaining always unfinished and imperceptible. I would usually forget about it as soon as I opened my eyes, leaving a feeling of sheer disappointment and dissatisfaction. Sometimes it reminded me of itself through another dream.

At first, a picture of an unknown riverbed rose before my eyes as if I were flying over it in a plane at a great height. Such dreams which impress us by high artistic value, purity, clarity of those pictures we observe. The next moment I felt I was standing on the bank of this river. The river is like any other river. It reminded me a little of our river Naryn in the middle of its current, a scenery around was quite ordinary, just some proportions were change, that made the picture unlike the Earth. The dream was like any other dream, almost real, if it weren't for the peculiar current of an impetuous river and excessive size of the hills around it.

I am afraid I've bothered you, so let us leave the subject till tomorrow, the more so I am approaching the culmination point and further the more spontaneous and disorderly my thoughts will become.

—Do not worry, Jolchuby,—I tried to comfort him. You have spoken just for an hour and a half, that is how long a usual lecture lasts, and we, if you remember, every day would have two or three such lectures, and then would go to laboratory and practical classes. If you are tired, you could have a rest 5-10 minutes to collect your thoughts before decisive assault.

Panoramic view of Tokyo

By the way, once I had too the similar dream. I was also flying by a plane over some wonderful town. This town stretched out near a wide auto route and consisted of just one huge house—colossal sky-scraper, as high and broad at the basic as our Sulayman-mountain. At the foot of it you could distantly see hundreds and thousands of cars, standing side by side at autoparks, while hundreds and thousands of other cars were skimming on both directions. This building of hundred of floors height and with millions of windows bore a remote resemblance with a modern passenger ship—it was a city-house of future, it couldn't be even compared neither with New-York, nor Tokyo, nor San-Francisco—surpassed them in size, so great and magnificence it was.

And only considerably later, having read in one scientific journal about city—sky-scraper's projects of the future on which American architects are working, I understood that my dream was prophetic, not just a fantasy. The most surprising thing was that this town was my native town Suzak, I think, a hundred years later.

—You are kidding! How did you guess?—Kerim expressed his doubt.

—I felt it in my heart,—said I.—Yes, it was my Suzak, changed beyond recognition, but I recognized it at once and bowed to its sublimate. It's one of the finest dreams presented me in my life.

—I also saw the future of my village in my dream once,—joined, ironically chuckling, Bolot.—And you Johnson, have a couple of apricots, they say it helps to think. But the future of my village was represented to me not in the sceneries, as yours, Sull, but in the faces of my acquaintances, my fellow-villagers, altered by time. They all were almost angel like, enlightened and ennobled by higher intellect. I won't say that my fellow-villagers are stupid, and defective people, but many of them lack many qualities, especially if we take into account that there's no limit to perfection. All of them—Ormotoy-aka, and Ulan, and Saipidin, and Kurchut-aba, and Kalbatyr, and Oskonbay and many others were the same, and recognizable at once, but at the same time, quite other people. Well, how to say that . . . any separate human being, both physically and spiritually is a more or less successful approachement of some strictly determined ideal. The closer to the ideal someone comes, the more beautiful, the fine he is, and vice versa the further one stands from ideal the less beautiful and perfect looked. So, in my dream all my acquaintances presented themselves in completely ideal transcendences, and I recognised them at once, but at the same time I did not recognize them, astonished by their perfection, by the diversity and richness of their new flourished beauty. One of them reminded me of James Bond, the other of Allan Delon, the third of Leonardo da Vinci, the fourth of Raphael, of Radge Kapur in his best years—I want to say that they were beautiful, elevated and noble and at the same time they remained my fellow-villagers, inimitable and unique in their individuality. Nobody in the village looked tired, irritated and displeased with himself and others, not saying about poor men, drunkards, failures and idlers. Even now I lay no claim on my villagers, I am quite pleased with them, but Ideal is Ideal and all of us are far staying from it—individually and in general aspect. It could not help frustrating you. But in that dream of mine everybody—brothers and not brothers, all sorts of uncles, aunts, aksackals[10]—were civilized, perfect, ennobled—spiritually and physically. There was a world of difference between present and this unreal appearances. "What a happy people! What a grand society! What a high degree of life performed such advantages!"— exclaimed I, infinitely proud for my people and at the same time not without envy looking at each perfectly new but the same time well recognisable face, as I am remained in the same condition, unchanged, my own disadvantages and demerits contrasted clearly out against such a refined society. But in reality most of my fellow-villagers, especially the youth, envied me—they saw Lady Fortuna standing at my side. I grew up in the town, graduated from the Institute, travelled a lot, whereas most of them had not such possibilities, they were brought up in large families, their parents were ignorant, they couldn't create the conditions, by which I was happy surrounded since childhood, because I was the only child in an intelligent family, having steady bounds with the countryside. But in the dream everything was quite the other way round: as if it was I, not they, who was brought up under difficult conditions, working hard the cotton plantation, suffering from villages discomforts and all sorts off absurdnesses, while all they did living under excellent conditions, was perfectionating themselves at the best educational establishments of the world. Their jobs were only creative ones, and it went on more fleetingly than on Japanese conveyor. And what about their rest and relaxation! We had never even dreamed of such relaxation! Yes, it was a marvellous dream and I was happy in that dream—not for myself, but for my countrymen, for their achievements; the more so as they were benevolent to me, they took me as I was, without any touch of arrogance, understanding that I was a product of a concrete epoch and nothing could be done about it. They were entirely different people, some celestial creatures. Can you imagine the bitter of awakening, a realisation that everything had been a dream, that in reality the things were different then they were before, and my countrymen were as they were in reality. In short, my native country remains the typical

---

[10]   aksackal—literally "white beard", old respected person

Kyrgyz country, conventionally difficult to alter things, to innovations and reforms—you could almost say this people live in deep lethargic sleep. And they were not likely to be awake in the next five years—to be changed radically for the better. Long decades and centuries will pass before we reach the most developed people of the world. But in my dream the quality of primarily material was so perfect and great, that there weren't any barriers and obstacles, which my native country could not overcome and push down.

Bolot's dream aroused everybody's interest, sometimes you have such dream when God himself seems speak to you.

Jolchuby was as pleased as we were, he stretched his big handpalm out to snake Bolot's hand before he came back to interrupted story.

—Everything I saw in my dream seemed at first to be something imagined, woven of different details, though it was not such a perfection as your marvellous dream, Bolot.

The river reminded me of my native Kyzyl-Suu, but it was wider and calmer. As for the houses and other buildings, scattered on the opposite bank—they were rather uncommon, they remotely ressembled the two-storied cottages that appeared recently on the coast of Issyk-Kul lake. Downstream the river grew narrow, winding as serpentine it passed along those gigantic hills,—here resemblance with the river Naryn was enhanced, especially that part between Toktogul and Kara-Kul towns. What I saw in that dream was like a creation of an artist gifted by cosmical imagination, conceived at first to paint the neighbourhood of Kara-Kul from the highest point of the town, and when his work had been half accomplished, he all of a sudden "rushed" to his favourite subject, with as result that he not only mixed west and east on canvas, but also gave the impression that the huge hills on the background were of unearthly origin and the picture had obtained a quite new cosmically sense and rate of impression.

It was a dream-conglomeration, the separate parts of which I saw at different times in the past, and I remembered, that long ago I saw both this river with unusual hills around, and those queer houses at the opposite bank. On the background behind the river there was a densely populated village, reminding me in the first place of the valley of Kara-Kul by it's relief. This obvious similarity was evidently connected with the experience of childhood. When I was only seven, I spent two wonderful months in Kara-Kul, which had made an incredible impression upon me. Even now it is my most favourite town in Kyrgyzstan, so clean, cosy, modern it is and at the same time virgin, stunning by the beauty of its landscapes.

At the second place you may notice that the riverside of Kyzyl-Suu reminds one by it's outline of the riverside of Kara-Kul, though, there's no electricity, and there are no modern buildings. But this was all just superficial similarity among details and objects well-known to me. In my dream I saw something, that neither Kara-Kul, nor Kyzyl-Suu could have. Among the outlines of houses and simple buildings there were beautiful buildings with gothic spires, high houses with steep slopes of roof untypical for our plane and poverty «every day» architecture. There were also some kinds of cottages, which are already known to us, but there (in my dream), they were much subtler and varied in form. You could see among them authentic masterpieces of architecture, at least they seemed so for us. Constructions of intricate forms, woven as a web—of very thick but firm eaves—some airy castles, galleries. Do you know the feeling when something is very important to you, as if you some divine mystery drifting, which you realise you simply cannot comprehend?

So did I, enjoying the pictures in this dream, as people enjoy perfect music, but when I remain my consciousness again and opened my eyes the tears were streaming down my cheeks. What was it? Who evoked such dreams? What an artist worried my soul? Where was he after? What subject is the main? Picturesque neighbourhoods of Kara-Kul and Kyzyl-Suu, merged together. Perhaps, it is the future of my country?—no, that's not the case, the details were as present one. Might it be a consequence of my affection of England—this Gothic spires, stone houses? It seemed to me that I saw this dream earlier, distinctly that I saw something like that, the river and a picturesque valley behind it I saw many years ago, at an age when I couldn't possibly imagine this all. I hadn't had such knowledge and impressions to dream of Gothic models. But then, at those cold winter nights in Kyzyl-Suu, I didn't have any idea of England, not even of the centre of the region where I lived. I was just a poor boy, locked up between the mountains since birth.

I would often jump up out of bed in the middle of night, trembling of contact with the beautiful, trying in vain to retain in memory scraps of marvellous sights, burning with desire to learn, to perceive what it had been, *until I became aware, that this dream was the same every time, it grew and developed as I grew and developed myself. It was like an award for the efforts, I did in order to catch at least a gleam of hope, to see on the riverbank a light cloud in the thick fog.*

This light arising in the fog was for me as the most cherished, dearest thing in the world. It seemed to me that my hopes, aspirations, the justification of my life depended on my ability to unravel this mystery. I rushed to the light with all my heart, as if experiencing all sufferings of recent years with new force. My innermost mystery was a few steps away from me, but I made a failure again. My dream dispersed like fog, as I managed to make just a step. Dreams always behave like that, breaking off at the most thrilling place, demanding new sacrifices for the sake of the next clue. I didn't achieve my aim, but I distinctly saw her stepping towards me.

It's just a wonder

**Thanks for your keen perceptiveness
and pleasure and kindness exceptional
for your descending and mercy.
Thanks for the deep and instant
understanding
what happened with me.**

It, s look really as if somebody
maybe great heaven
prepared and honed
every part of your soul
so precious, close and congruent
with mine in every details and wholly,
in the basic things, stems moods and core
that I am truly astonished now—
why we were so long searching each other
on the face of not so big Globe.
It's just a wonder,
my best beloved

that our dreams conjoined
after such long sojourns.

XIII

All my investigations didn't just intensify, but absorbed
me totally in the explosion of hard work, which had astonished
many people even before. Then it became almost monstrous, as
if in me some hidden appalling forces had been awakened, forces
like thermonuclear energy, whose secret rules I began to master. I
understood that the power of human mind is limitless, within a
short time I apprehended the deep secrets of parapsychology, higher
mathematics, the theory of light; I understood, that the theory of
relativity had a much more universal character, embracing not only
the physical world but also spiritual essence, the cosmos, the speed
of human thinking which efficiency is almost equal to the speed of
light, we experienced the same as during physical motion at enormous
speed: the world around us unravelled its secrets, and we perceived
its fundaments in that flight fly further—to the most remote future
and even beyond its limits, obtaining immortality directed at light.
And then there's nothing impossible for us and nothing inaccessible,
the most wonderful, unrealisable dream begins to embody in reality,

the most impudent gust of fantasy come true all of a sudden. That days all my life turned into continuous revelation, into a sparkling flow of inspiration, different ideas, surmises and enlightenments were trustfully surrounding me, they were crying out to be written down in my scientific notebooks and I absorbed them insatiable, enjoyed their beauty and freshness and went on taking up new ideas. It was not scientifical fame or career that attracted me, all my attempts were aimed at unveiling the biggest mystery in my life.

. . . The distance between me and this "light", moving in fog on the bank of the river shortened steadily step by step, dream by dream.

. . . Little by little we were moving towards each other, and gradually some silhouette, as if under an artist's brush took more and more distinct shape. When I approached it closer finally, the scales seemed to fall from my eyes. Remember that everything was going on in a dream which repeated itself once or twise a year and which required of me an incredible energy. The following happened all of a sudden, as allway after a night of hard working. In front of my eyes appeared a smiling fascinating girl in white. Her hair was light, a little curly, thrown back by the wind, she was all light, purity and radiance, as if she was made of light, of that cloud on the bank of the river. I saw her with unusual clarity and distinctness, as if thousands of suns were illuminating our rendezvous, and recognized her at once, from the first sight, as well as she recognized me, even if we had never and nowhere met before.

But nevertheless we met, recognized each other—two little human beings, lost among millions of other destinies and people, looking for each other in an unimaginable, boundless ocean, in a cosmos of millions of other visions and dreams. Oh, we managed to perform impossible and the cause of it were our hearts which long time ago, since childhood, or perhaps even earlier,—we ought to ask about it professor Hokins, working over the formula for each human life and fate, beginning from the Day of creation and till Doomsday—our hearts persistently had been paving a way through to each other, sending mysterious signals, known only to them, losing and finding again the signs, rejoicing and despairing, which at last opened our eyes to everything and let us to this rendezvous.

Yes, it was our first rendezvous in dream, just a few moments, during which we only managed to make two or three steps along the river, hand in hand, but which threw so much light upon our lives.

I saw her against the background of her home, and she saw me against the house of my aged parents. It was the merging of our two dreams, more than that, the merging of two revelations, some dual illumination, in which relatives of both sides of the mirror were reflected: as if I saw a piece of her native England behind her, and she saw my Kysyl-Suu behind me. Thus a new reality came into reality in the world of dreams, where everything was familiar to me from the cradle, and at the same time there was much unknown to me before, not at all strange, but fine and dear, as sudden and full clue of my continuous troubles, dim searches and desires.

This "illumination" was so powerful and bright, that that moment the most innermost secrets of nature seemed to lay bare before our eyes, and that very moment was as an instant of the most full and profound happiness. Behind her I saw not only her house, but also persons dear to her, relatives, I saw things which were special dear to her, and I seemed to perceive what troubled and worried her most. The same was going on with her; as well as I did she examined carefully my background behind me. Using the language of mathematics, it was dual mutual reflection—the dream, it was redemption for my unsleepy nights, agonizing doubts, searches,— dream, *which was even greater than the very reality, giving birth to it.*

But the dream dispelled before I could manage to say something. I understood that there was nothing I could do about it but to begin everything from the very beginning, to tune myself to the search of new signals, coming from outside, to produce such impulses by myself and catch their reflections. Every day, every hour and even every minute I thought of her. I hang pictures and maps of Great Britain in my room around. I worked hard day and night, I was burning myself and the career of young promising mathematician down, everything was cancelled for an uncertain time. I had to start everything from the very beginning and approximately in half a year I established a telepathic communication again. In the dream I managed to talk to her. I asked her "What is your name?" To which she answered: "Call me by the name of your favourite song, if you find me, my destiny will change . . . and then you'll know my real name,"—and that moment I awake . . . Two days I cracked my brains over these puzzling words, remembering the sad expression on her face. What it could mean? I began even to get angry with her, why she decided to speak in riddles when everything surrounding us seemed to be a big puzzle and I had no idea how to get out of that. But then I comprehend, that there's no guilt from her side, not a shadow of flirt—only an iron logic of hidden telepathic contact, where, like that in ordinary life you pay in real blood for every step up, for every revelation. One early morning the marvelous effect touched me again. I do not remember what exactly I dreamed of, perhaps I didn't dream at all, but at dawn I heard one of my favourite melodies of "Beatles"—the song "Eleanor Rigby" ringing in my ears. I awoke as though I was drifting on the waves of this music, I comprehended and felt acutely all the depth as never before— do you remember the song of a girl, who lived in a small English village, about her sad fate? How she diligently visited church where the priest instilled her to obedience and resignation. So she grew so obedient, accurate, not missing a single prayer day, hoping that she would find her happiness one day, that she would deserve it. But she didn't wait till what the priest promised her,—instead of that one day a coffin with her dead body was carried into the same church, and over her body studded with flowers the same priest, that catcher of souls, read his prayer. The song finishes up on heartbreaking note— the singer, this golden voiced McCartney exclaims: *where is the person, who could save you from oblivion and death? how many people on Earth like you were deceived—who would save them all?*

The text was rather powerful, isn't it, and God indoubdlessly created us for actively life. So my girl, she is Eleanor Rigby. If I'll fail to find her—her destiny will be as sad as in this song but If I'll have enough courage to tear her out of obscurity and uncertainty, if our rendezvous won't only happen in the dream, but in reality too,—then I'll learn her real name and her destiny will be different, unlike that the of Eleanor Rigby. This is what was the meaning of her words.

XIV

Later, I had this dream again, and we managed to complete the most difficult and impossible. We appointed a rendezvous, that time not in a dream, but in reality.

As soon as I heard the exact date, place and time of the date everything disappeared. I understood, that the dream wouldn't be repeated again, its mission was fulfilled and an ordinary reality began for both of us.

—And where are you to meet and when?

—In 4 months in Moscow, on the Red Square at the monument to Minin and Pojarsky, on 20th of October, at 15 o'clock Greenwich or at 18 o'clock Moscow time, in 1984.

—Or at 21 o'clock our time—whispered Kerim.—Look here, why on 20th of October? Couldn't you make appointment for an earlier date?

—As I've already said, the dream has its own rules and logic. Even to become yourself aware yourself in a dream, that is to feel that you are sleeping and just having a dream is a formidable task, requiring an immense concentration of will. Let alone appointing a date during your dream, which is to happen in reality. We didn't just agree to meet, but—we blessed for this right through much suffering, we got information of both place and time of rendezvous in some kind of instant enlightenment, to which we could change nothing.

—Yes, it is interesting,—said Bolot in a low voice,—it is obvious, that the Red Square is evidently the most appropriate dating place, like a support signal, orientation point, beacon for consciousness in transition from the unsteady and shapeless state of dreaming into reality. Oh! I understand! that girl might have set her mind on visiting our country, at that very moment, perhaps, and she just had no chance to come in the near future.

—It will be all right, if so—said Kerim.—As for our Jolchuby he isn't likely to have such a chance even in five years. I mean the possibility to visit England. It is to difficult for simple people. Well, she is coming to the date herself, she felt probably what kind of a man you are, you won't move in anyway. Ya, that's how things go. It is a masterpiece, even if it is just fib and a lie, give me your hand, buddy, but do not squeeze it, please.

—I think so too,—smiled Bolot.—Everything is thought out so well, that you won't have the heart to call it a lie. No, I feel, that there is something in it, some rational kernel, if there is a lie, then this lie is even higher than truth itself surely, your girl understands at heart, guesses, that even if you lose your head falling in love with her, you won't visit England. Because we are all living inside of well protected and guarded country confined 7th part of world.

—That's it!—interfered Kerim,—What the hell! A girl comes first to the rendezvous. What kind of boy is he, waiting for his girl sitting at home. If I were at your place I would all the same appoint a date with her somewhere in London, say under the tower of Big Ben. Just out of principle, you see? Even if I had less chances than you. When the time comes, we'll see it. Love doesn't know any bounds and borders.

—That girl learned much about me. She thanked me.

—Thanked you? For what, I wonder? For coming to you herself?—Kerim couldn't stop.

—For the dreams we experienced together,—quietly, almost in a whisper uttered Jolchuby, paying no attention to Kerim's tone.

—All right, and what are we supposed to do?

—This is just what I come to you for. Give me advice, please. Tell me what to do?

—What to advise, if she is coming to you herself? Meet her in Moscow, bring her right to Kyzyl-Suu. Nothing to doubt about! An ordinary affair. Introduce her to your old men: "I ask you to be kind and gracious to us". Establish a bridge between Albion and Kyzyl-Suu, you say? OK, wish you good luck.

But Jolchubai didn't seem to be paying attention to him, he returned to his innerworld again. As for us we were getting cracked of fatigue.

—Hey, give me your hand!—Bolot stretched his, very big one,—and our two giants shook each others hands.

—Bolot solemnly delivered:

—Ladys and gentlemens! I ask all of you to stand up and bow your head. Can't you understand, that we face a historical fact, accomplished just now. Our close friend has performed something heroical. He is the greatest from all well-known travellers to the land of fantasy and dream, a real Columbus, discovering his own America, isn't it? We suspected him of that kind of things before, but not to that extent: we just thought that he would become some professor or academic, but . . . who knew the way everything has happened. Jolchuby excelled us not only as a reformer of the law of physics, but he's turned over all our former notions of time, space, consciousness and dream. I believe you, Jolchuby, believed you in the past too, but now, if you like, I'll stand as your shadow? By the way, did you inform your parents of it?

Jolchuby didn't answer at once, but sighed.

—This is the gist of the affair,—he stared at the floor, his hands placed on his head. He tousled his hair and became even more dishevelled, then all of a sudden he turned and looked at us with his gogle eyes. Seeing this swift metamorphoses I thought he would have been a rather attractive man, if he could more carefully control himself. He was very eccentric, you know.

—You see, my parents are mere countrymen. They haven't been anywhere in their lifetime, they spent all life in Kyzyl-Suu, in the mountains. They went down even to the centre of the region very rarely.

—Well, what is in it all? They are not the only ones in the village who haven't seen the world! So they will see it now,—I felt that something was wrong there.

—There are nine of us, children, in the family. Although I am not the oldest, I am the third, like a second father, as no one is likely to have such an opportunity to study at the Institute in future.

—Come to the point. We know this ourselves. What do you want to say with that?

—Consequently, this girl and me have not else cohesive circumstances where we could live together,—the voice of Jolchuby broke off.

—Well, how to say . . . Our time hasn't come yet, that's why it will be better if this love never comes true, I mean, it never leaves that magic world, where it was destined to be born and flourish. It seems to me, that she is not strong enough to carry this heavy burden.

—What crap are you uttering?—Kerim rose from his place.— You, you feel ashamed for your native land! Just look at him, what a brick he is! You are well aware that I hate this sort of dribble persons, I bet you're not stronger than I am. If you want to know, most evil on earth happens through the fault of such people as you, through their indifference to everything, through their shame for everything, they would sell even their own fathers if they have a chance, they could even play dirty tricks on their Motherland, and what is most offensive, they wouldn't even feel it, realize it, and there will always be people to support and think of them as decent.

—I never feel shame at all,—uncertainly objected Jolchuby.—But nevertheless, it is very difficult question.

—Nothing can be done about it,—it is love, which is suffering,— said Bolot.—Some ancient philosopher compared love with a battle, saying, that one must prepare to love as well as to the war in order to go through all losses. Only then you have a chance to win.

—Thank you for your truthful words. It is not without reason that your head resembles in its shape a head of future man, who is clever. But it's time to come to the point. Let us make up a plan of battle operations once we are challenged, imagine, that we are Napoleon, who at such cases saw the tree on the whole and each leaf of it separate. Let's take these western capitalistic regimes by storm. Don't be scared, Jolchuby. We understand you well. Your love is our honour,—saying those words Kerim got so excited that he stood up.

—The matter is, my friends, to show our land and its inhabitants in a positive light. Am I right? It'll be some kind of exhibition for your bride. Don't be scared, buddy, we're not as backward as we perhaps seem to be, the sixth part of the Earth to shirk some small Island. Everything will be all right. If there is a need, we would just take bosoms each and begin to sweep off all dirt from our lives, to put order in it, set ourselves right. You see, Jolchuby, we'll involve in our campaign everything and everybody: from the untidy streets of our town to little imps, our younger brothers; we will steadily and systematically get rid of everything old, sluggish and obsolete, which haven't died yet, but continue to poison our lives discomposingly; we'll perfect and educate each other and other people around us. If it's necessary, we'll crush everything obsolete and out of-date standing in our way. What will we be ashamed of? Of our own slackness! We'd better strive for happiness and attain it not only in our dreams! Don't you be bored to death by this ephemeric existence, when you are not a captain of your life? If we don't blow up this passivity, put an end to it once and forever, then we'll never reach that high level of life, which highly developed and highly civilised countries have reached,— we would vegetate for a long time in our unsolved problems, provincialism, stupidness, savageness, laziness, impracticality of most people, especially authorities, who are more afraid of possible awakening from this awful somnolence, as it is easier for a sleepy half-alive leader to govern completely sleepy people. Let's announce a war on it and never be embarrassed to see things as they are and call them, consequently by their names, no matter how difficult it will be. Surely, it is formidable affair, I guess we'll meet a strong resistance, people more experienced and clever, but less courageous will laugh at us and smirk behind our backs, not saying of swearing and threads, which will fall thick and fast on us from all sides, but we will overcome that all and be winners, finding a great number of like-minded people.

—That is enough for today,—Bolot rose to his feet, ignoring excited Kerim, ready to go further like that.—Let's drop this subject till tomorrow. Today we had a substantial conversation, imagine: more than four hours we have talked about a dream. But as they say, a dream is just a dream, and you can't indulge in your dream too excessively, even if it is your greatest dream you have been fostering from cradle. A dream, if you want to know, is as a woman: she wants to obey us, so is her nature, and only then she will be happy.

I liked this philosophical ending of the host, it made an impression on Kerim as well,—really, what a right thought he had expressed, at a proper time, and place—we all were very tired of our long trip to the world of dream. Not each of us was as quick to grasp as our Jolchuby. Jolchuby would understand everything at subconscious level, even when the lecturer didn't manage to open his mouth, just was thinking it over. However, this time even he got exhausted he was just sitting relaxed on the sofa, without lifting his head, or perhaps, he was pulling himself together to make a next rush into a world unknown to anybody, which could open to let only Jolchuby in. But no . . . it was enough, at least for today. Meanwhile, in the kitchen there was a luxurious plov, waiting for us,—a real masterpiece, with all species and greens,—which took a burden from our minds, which made us forget all described dizzy problems, giving each of us a fine relaxation, as enjoying this plov and drinking green tea it was impossible to talk of something else but just this.

The magic of love

My favorite star
on the darkest sky.
Your light is coming to me
throught abrest of times
and cold distances,
measured by millenniums
of light years travel.
Yes, what has observed right now
and inspired me
in the sky above
had belonged to ancient times,
when had lived Ramses and Nefertary

my love.

But why the star
so impressed me
if all I have seen and inspired right now
coming to me from deadly far distance?
For what reason my heart so strongly abscessed?

Because love as a thought
has broken out all basic physics laws,
she primarily occupied all space
around us,
and really was born with universe
from the one superhottest point, my pleasure,
so our feels conquered world instantly and completely
and not respect the dictates of times, distances and other measures.

That's why
when I look for you
my heart know you feel me
that I love you
right now.
That is exactly truly fact
according with quantum theory
and I verify it soon,
my favorite star
on the darkest sky.

Part two

The great hit of master[11]

It's really hit of great Master,
when million others just a dreamwaster . . .
Try you too to find in dream where deployed the largest empire
and then a town in its area

---

[11] In the 1982 years, after many experiments, preparedness and hard
working in various branch of sciences—Jolchuby was very gifted
person—he found out through dreams his passion, dear one and alone
in this world, communicate with them in dreams and have agreed
with her to meet in reality, marked precise coordinates and time for
first appointment. Red Squere in Moskow and Kremlin, served as
orientir for our dreamweaver when they pointed right place and time
for meeting in their dreams

How it was happen? I dont know but this chap done it. I am also trying
very hard to find my love in my dreams but can not to do it.

and a street in the town
and a home and a window
of the room where grown and wait you
so carefully hidden by the times and distances
yours dearest one—yours love indispensable
the perfect one created for you and no one else.
This hero did it—find the love and save her
from sharp talons of forlornness.

I could not done that
to find and save my ultimate love
that would waiting for me all her life in vain
somewhere, maybe, in south latitudes . . .
As a great number of persons around the world
worth not for honor of Love and hers blesses
could not to find, calculate and win his real passion.
But Jolchuby did that
He found his soul mate—not as we are all,
the millions Romeo's of losses and wastes
so he is really great hero in history
who explained, resolved and won the love's mystery.

I

How good, that there is such a wonderful thing as sleep—simple, humane, quiet. When one can merely dive into its waters, sleep deeply as it is, without any telepathic tricks, in order to wake up the next morning very fresh, as if born again, even if you have unloaded a full wagon of problems and couldn't stand on your legs from exhaustion,—in the morning you wouldn't find a single trace of it, you can briskly take up your work again. Do sleep, if you want to achieve something, I would say.

Slept out for an hour longer than usual, we attacked Jolchuby with a new force. We put the question point-blank,—perhaps, buddy, you are kidding us? Perhaps you want to make fun of us?—take care, buddy. We'll believe you, but if it turns out that you are deceiving us—we won't feel pity for you, you'll be deprived of your bright head, see? We won't forgive such a trick, see?—Forget it, Kerim, I tell you, on 20 of October, at 3.p.m. Greenwich my fate will be at stake, go with me and make sure of it yourself.—And what if your beloved won't be able to come, Johnson? Anything may happen: the plane, perhaps, would be delayed, or workers of the airport would be on strike right on October, and you don't know her address, do you? So in such a case you'd never meet; wait a minute, can't you return to telepathy again? All right, you can but it will take a lot of time and efforts, and by the way, you will not succeed it that time, as each phenomenon is unique—in any case, we should seize the chance. Your girl seems to be smart, understands everything in her heart, once she promised, she is bound to come, it is in the nature of English character—the heavier the press of life circumstances, the more persistent they become, approaching their aim. It wouldn't be bad, if our fellow-countrymen would adopt such qualities, because they are used to follow the way of least resistance, dancing around the manger day and night. So, if the rendezvous fails, it would only be our own fault, I am sure rain, hail, frost, snow—a bad weather in short—that kind of things may happen only in our country. They have another climate, both economical and political; so do not wonder, Johnson, if our trains and planes be out of order, wouldn't fly, tickets would be unavailable and so on. Then reach Moscow even if you have to ride a horse,—hm, a wonderful idea!—and what if even this horse would refuse as well?—then cycle your way along Kazakhstan's steppes on a push-cycle, or go on foot or crawl on all four, but get there on time!

After such a stormy debates we made a decision to take our leaves all together. But it was not an easy thing to do. Only Kerim chief let him go at once. As for me, I had to take some pains, not because of my chief's obstinacy, but because of my colleagues: there was no one to replace me, so I had to ask them to take over my work. But it was difficult for Bolot most of all: his boss turned out to be a hard man, who doesn't give you any freedom, no matter what happens to you—even if a Martian himself was going to call on you, on whom the destiny of our planet would depend, it's of no importance, either do what you are to do, or leave . . . Yes, Bolot had to let himself be fired. Understanding the situation, we tried to persuade him that we could manage without him, though it would be a great loss—to lose a man of the future, when you are about to undertake something really important. But Bolot wouldn't listen to us, confirming, that it was even better that he was fired as he had been looking for another, more perspective job.

❚❚

First of all we started from Jolchuby's native ail, small village, each of us providing ourselves with a "big besom", burning of desire to put it in proper order.

On arriving to Kyzyl-Suu we cautiously announced, that some guests from far away were going to visit us. The first reaction of the hospitable villagers was, of course, one of joy; they smiled, nodded their heads, and some of them felt at once, that this guest was the fiancee of Jolchuby,—and you did not believe in telepathy? By the way it's no wonder to feel it, when four young men arrive to ail and spoke about some guests, but nevertheless, we tried to conspire everything, deliberately misleading the most sage of them, putting their secret "investigation apparatus" on the false trail—saying that we were not ourselves properly informed about, what quests were coming, but that there were distinct directions from the side the communist party and the government (these two words used to make the most powerful impression on Kyzyl-Suu's inhabitants), and that they in no case should make themselves ashamed.

On the other hand, we were to be especially careful and tactful in respect to Jolchuby and his relatives, trying to exclude possibility of emotional traumas, even the slightest, as our friend was under the cross-fire. From one side we, from the other—inhabitants of Kyzyl-Suu. Actually, I consider rudeness and mockery to be the first enemies and ruiners of love. Let's recollect our childhood, what love, what affection, what impulses would be born in our adolescently tender and singing souls, what girls, what babies and princesses would we fall in love with, but all our finest feeling were eradicated by grins, irony, mockery of our close relates—so we grew up betraying ourself, betraying the best we had by nature, fearing to be revealed, to be ashamed, if you had happened to fall in love with some girl. Even now that we have grown up and have become stronger physically as well as spiritually, even though we can defend our feelings now, we nevertheless turn into children again every time we fall in love becoming helpless, defenceless.

Taking all those nuances into consideration we surrounded Jolchuby with a solid wall of care. We carried on an ingenious combinative on the land of Kyzyl-Suu, pulling the wool over anybody and everybody eyes on behalf of our best intentions, little by little approaching our main aim. That will do, Asyrankul—aka, what fiancee are you talking about? what girl would agree to marry us, having graduated from the institute only the other day, who would let us marry his daughter for nothing? If you are so conserned, why don't you help us with kalyng[12], the rest we would arrange ourselves, or perhaps you can help us to find a girl? Oh, no, she won't do, take her for yourself as a second wife, what? Ouch! who says that town-girls are cheaper? Oh, no, you are mistaken town girls are hard to handle, they know their rights, they wouldn't let anyone rule over them. That'll do Asyrankul-aka, you'd better tell me, can I taste your kymyz[13]? All right then, I'll drop in the evening, if I am free. Ah! Apsatar, it's you? Hello, How's life? I'm all right, and you? I heard you became father for the second time, sorry, couldn't come to congratulate you, by the way, aren't you expecting a third child? No? Right you are, it's such an enormous task, that it is not enough just to give birth to a child, you ought to properly bring him up. And how many children are you planning to have, if it's not a secret? I guess five, it will be good, isn't it? or you want a bit more? All right, it's your business, you may have even ten of them, and become a father-hero, I'd just wish your ten

---

12   kalyng—the price the parents of the groom pay for the bride
13   kymyz—fermented mare's milk

times happiness. Who is it, you ask? It's Sultan, don't you see? He is here for the third time. And this is Bolot, meet him. Well, we have to go, our regards to your wife. What? Hunting? Surely, we'll go! Just get a gun and plenty cartridges. No, not tomorrow, we have some work to do. We'll meet later.

In general, we created quite a grand stir in Kyzyl-Suu, we said to our fellow-countrymen that now many people from all over the world are becoming interested in our country, both in its the beauty of the nature and in its people. The villagers were glad to hear our words, as the kyrgyzes like to receive guests. Then we cautiously hinted at the fact that guests we expected were highly cultured and educated people and what was the most important, that they had a high opinion of Kyzyl-Suu's inhabitants. Someone took some pain to convince them that life in Kyzyl-Suu is a paradisical, to praise everything mountain-high. Oops, Abdymanap, who told you that we thought it is not so? Kyzyl-Suu is really good, it can't be different, judge for yourself, would we come to this place if we didn't love it. That is the reason why we are here, dear villagers, is to make a village representable for such unusual guests.

Good-natured villagers agreed to it, they understood, that the situation to come was really delicate, but when we demanded what had to be done for three months, they were greatly surprised. Ohu!. what is it? they are coming only in three months? then why you trouble us so early? Are the guests so important, that we have to prepare three months before? Hm, but once you beg us, though, we'll do all you ask, Jolchuby, my dear, only yesterday you were as small as a thimble, and today, you've grown-up into a fine tall fellow, arrived in Kysyl-Suu to teach us how to live. Well, very well, don't forget to drop in to see us with your friends, to say "hello" to your uncle, he'll be glad, and on such an occasion I'll make you such tasty kattama[14] as nobody else can make, Jolchuby. If you don't manage today, then come tomorrow, otherwise your uncle can get offended, as he is rather old now.

---

[14]   kattama—specially prepared bread with oil and sugar

In general, we walked through Kysyl-Suu, meeting different people—not only acquaintances and relatives but also people unknown to us, enjoying their boundless hospitality, throwing off all shyness, meddling in their mode of life, trying to find out what they eat, how they live, how they spend their free time, observing closely the interiors of their kitchens, bedrooms, nurseries, living rooms. Of course we didn't tell all of them about the expected guests. Sometimes we got to some houses under the pretext of data collection. It was right that we decided not to restrict ourselves just to the "inspection" of Jolchuby's relatives, if we wanted inspect, then we should inspect every house, as we can hardly trick the relatives of Jolchuby's bride, when they arrive in Kysyl-Suu in their luxurious limousines, rolls-royce and mercedeses, if we show them only houses and yards prepared beforehand. Englishmen, our future matchmakers, may object to it categorically and say—no, no, this is not what we want to see, we want to see it by ourselves, by our eyes, to knock on the first door we meet—what'll happen then? Can they be blamed for this well-known capitalistic characteristic? And what if the first house they happen to meet is the house of this profligate Kanky, or of someone else, not less "respectable citizen" of Kysyl-Suu? He would make the whole ail ashamed! Or maybe, we should warn Kanky not to show himself in the street, if foreigners drive up to his house?—Indeed! He is not the person to be talked out, he appears usually where he is least of all desired and makes such a mess! And what if we try to persuade him with a bottle of vodka?—Oh! It is an idea, then he would sit at home the whole month, if necessary. But he is not alone in Kuzul-Suu. We will need a lot of vodka for satisfying all of them. Yes, it is hard problem. I think the Caucasians can be considered as the best at hospitality. Can you believe me, Bolot, three months ago I switched on the TV set, there was evening of Rasul Gasmatov's poetry on Ostankino in Moscow. The poet himself was reciting his poems in presence of two or three thousand poetry-lovers. So, at the end of that evening the poet invited them all to his native land Dagestan, on his father's anniversary, announcing the exact date; and he invited not only the audience sitting in the hall of Ostankino, but also all TV watchers, including you and me. Just imagine, it was the first channel of Central TV, prime-time after the program "Vremya"—100-150 million of people as minimum. That's what you call a real man. And then he added in the end not to worry, there would be enough rooms and places for everyone!

And what might saying about us? We can't even decide how to receive the guests from a tiny Island in the North Sea. Eh, Jolchuby, if you had such authority and weight as Rasul Gasmatov has, no doubt, you would not only invite all Central TV watchers, but would also ask them to send your invitation to all their friends and relatives, who couldn't manage to see you on TV. Can you imagine, how amazing it would sound!

The small town in England, calling Darlton.

III

We approached different people in different ways. With some of them we spoke frankly, stating the very point, with others we would turn everything into mockery, making them laugh and laughing ourselves, but it was a bitter laughter, very often we would lose control then we began speaking without twists and turns,—haw long will we stay so stupid, remain such bunglers with complacent, glossy faces, when will we change these quilted, smoked through trousers for something more convenient and modern? Can't we really live and work properly? The public bath-house doesn't work, you say? There isn't any water? Its boiler was out of order from the very beginning? aha, there you are! making errors from the very beginning, but even if it is so, why don't you build your own bath-house, not reckoning on the sluggish and slow state. What? You don't have enough bricks? Is it a problem for such an experienced builder as you are, Abdurazak, who worked for a building battalion once, when you served in Soviet Army, didn't you? Imagine that "ded"[15] orders you to build a bath-house within a week, how, what—that's your problem. If it comes to that, face it with masonry, since you live on the bank of the river, use the opportunity, it would stay for centuries as some monument to the cleanliness and culture of our age!

We had to scare some people to death by means of command-administrative system because of inefficiency of other methods. Imaging one day some state committee arrives in our village, trying to shift out those persons, who don't read books, in order fine them for a fairly big sum. Then we spread a rumour that those who don't read books at all would be photographed and their pictures would be published in "Chalkhan", "Mushtum", or even "Crocodile"[16] with appropriate disgraceful term, that would scare them even more.

—And what books are we to read?—Hm, well. Shakespeare, I think, you know such a great writer? No? Then you'll fail. If you knew anything of Shakespeare you'd get out, as the members of this committee revere this Shakespeare. He is as a god for them. Find and

---

[15] ded—In Soviet Army soldiers were informally divided into "deds"(grandpa) and "salagas"(little boy) according to length of their stay. "Salagas" were to obey "deds" in everything and very often cruel treated and suffered.

[16] "Chalkhan", "Mushtum", "Crocodile"—the names of popularly soviet satirically magazines.

read the books written by him—they are available in any library. Read other authors as well. Every evening, after penning your cattle do spend two or three hours reading and take books with you when you go to pasture your sheeps! In a year you'll become as wise as Solomon! The most beautiful girls will hang around your neck. Think yourself: why would people be so eager to enter Institutes and Universities? Just to get education? And if you don't read, you do not make any progress, you will like raw skin, good only to wipe feet at.

Some of Kysyl-Suu's fine fellows were to be threatened even more, but we prudently refrained, fearing possible complications. We helped to some of Kysyl-Suu's inhabitants, for example, to Abylgazy-aka, to finish building of his bath—house, if it hadn't been for us he would be still lingering on. It was only the third or the fourth bath-house in a village with a population of two or three thousands. The only public bath-house built recently was out of service. Collecting enough courage we frankly asked—Israil-agay and other representatives of the intelligence—sorry, agay, but we are wondering how long has it been since the teachers took care of their appearances, look what a gait they have, a shepherd is more graceful than your teachers! And your women, how they are dressed! No, you don't understand me, I don't mean poverty of cloths, on the contrary, teachers in Kysyl-Suu seem to be fairly wealthy, I mean taste, sense of proportion, strictness, you understand? How can such a person, who didn't bring himself up, who can't know how to dress, behave, walk can teach and bring children up? Even pupils look more accurate than their teachers. Aren't you ashamed of yourself to appear unshaved in front of the classes? And what's wrong with my long hair? I can let it grow as I take care of it and you perhaps are eager to shave my head, aren't you? But indeed, in such a hole, like Kysyl-Suu it's better to be without hair, there's neither bath-house, nor hairdresser, nor hot water. It is pointless to resent me, as I tell you the naked truth for your own sake, were I your enemy—I would lavish praises. You'd better join us, help us to bring our campaign to an end.

Do you want your progeny to remember your name? So, try your best to get out of that filth, in which we are up to the neck. It wouldn't be bad at all if everybody tried to improve and perfect himself, both the old and the young generations. Surely these are difficult questions, as our aksackals aren't used to be taught by youth as we are. But as for country youth, they are to pay a price in particular, they must give up most of their wild habits. Why can't they be such fine-fellows as Choton. So cheerful, lively, smart. Has anyone ever seen him gloomy or bad-tempered? It is impossible. And so mobile: today he is here, tomorrow he is in Osh, Frunze, Naryn, then he flies to Moscow or even further. Where is he now, by the way? In Jalal-Abad? Oh, just as I've predicted! And when he'll be back? No one knows when. I seem to know how to call him back. Arrange ulak[17] in Kysyl-Suu and I bet, he will come at once from whenever he happens to be. He is born for this game and can forget the rest of the world playing it, he can even restrain his passion for travelling and discoveries. Eh! I fear you will suffer from your incredible sluggishness and passiveness. You forgot no pains, no gains. Your dzhigit[18] will disperse all over the world, and your girls will leave such an uncosy, maladjusted to modern life ail, and the burden of your interior problems will grow and grow, caused by slavery of everyone, by lack of elementary conditions, and a day may come when sons turn away from their fathers and brothers from their brothers, what will happen then? You can be angry with me because of my words, Kulchetin, but I'll say, nevertheless, I don't like most of your patriarch views. Here it would be right to say: "If your body is clean, then your soul is pure, and human happiness depends much on such important things, as warm water, bath, well-groomed yard, well-built house. And among our intelligence there is such a fraternity, people who are just ready to cry out of love for their home, ails, consider ail's customs almost ideal, but this is love from far away, when you live in town, enjoying all goods of civilisation, professing a quite different moral. Why, they arrive to the ails usually just to enjoy your hospitality, not at all inclined to help you. Surely, we could have behaved the way they did and deserve their complimentary opinion by that, but we climbed up the wall of our own free will, and most probably we set them against ourselves at last.

---

[17]   ulak—kyrghyz national game
[18]   dzhigit—young, brave person

Let's go to live forever

Let's go, dear, to live together
and we should look eventually
what happen with such decision,
certainly we are growing fast older and downgraded
going to end, my sugar candy,
but we have been together,
that s sound finely, doesn't?

So let's keep living together.
No one warranted
what happened from such idea:
would we live in peace and harmony
or our life have been hurly-burly,
the whole one endless cacophony,
maybe we are both drown
with tsunami of troubles and problems
or we shall find way for harbor
our safety and harmony,
or our ship will moved to divorcee
and fighting for shearing joint collecting property.
No one know answers for that hellish questions
and predict future possibilities and revelation
in all its damned variations,
maybe love will thousand times cursing
and regretting and lamenting
for this occasion and acceptance
of long waiting meeting, suggestion and dance.

But let's keep living together
right now and without any postponing
traying never miss each other's
and we are looking for what's happened later,

growing older and downgrade
but we have been live with you together
my dear sugar candy,
let's, please, living forever.

IV

Things didn't seem to be going right. The burden we heaved on our shoulders turned out to be so heavy, that we soon began to lose our ardour.

Some got our point and were ready to help or just support us, while the others got so cross with our remarks, that they wished us to hell, but tolerated us, gnashing their teeth, because we were their guests. Still others would nevertheless fly into a temper when after stormy debates we would politely offer him irons to press his trousers—they would be at the point of flinging the very iron at us. And how many looked askance at us "do you come from the Moon, guys?" and whispering to themselves "away with you and your quests . . ." Had we tried something like that in another village, we'd been torn into pieces for sure, and Kysyl-Suu was said to be stronghold of hospitality not without reason, there a guest would be allowed everything. But nevertheless, their patience as well as our seemed to be come to an end. The most distressing things were the meetings with that sort of people who would agree to everything, nod heads, approve of our plans—but if at that very moments we would have happened to catch expressions of their eyes, taking a detached view, we would have been astonished at their colourless blankness, as if they were not alive at all: you come to them in order to work, willing to help them, and they just smile at you making sugarsweet faces, and go on nothing, only nods and smiles. They were fully deprived of pride and dignity: not a bit of a human being, but made of clay, nothing to do about that.

On the other hand, as ill luck would have it Jolchuby happened to be born in Kysyl-Suu, the most backward and undeveloped parts of Kyrghyzstan. You are unlikely to meet another village like it in our region. You won't believe me, but electrification of Kysyl-Suu was completed only in the beginning of the eighties, that is, only five years ago. Due to its remoteness from the district centre and the bad quality of the mountain roads the ail had been isolated from the rest world for a fairly long period, so it had been stewing in its own juice and almost got savage, especially in comparison with other villages.

And there were also such people indeed, who tried to give us the full responsibility for such an unfavourable state of things in Kyrghyzstan, "e-eh . . . If you are so conscious, if you are so worried about the life of local people, then make the direct transport communication between Kysyl-Suu and district centre be adjusted. Ya, there's a road, and a bus which comes in time. But why don't we get long-distance buses on our roads?" So they ordered, as if one of us had been at least the chief of the bus base. And what was the most surprising the people who asked us that were people, whose positions in ail's society were higher than those of the rest.

They had real authority, such as a chief zootechnician, accountant, engineer and even Party organiser of the local state governing. They were many times more powerful than we, but nevertheless, any time we talked about business they shifted work upon us, asking us to help them with one or the other work, as if the state farm had nothing to do with that and as if the four of us could solve all problems, which a state farm with its three thousand workers couldn't solve. But when it came to the point, when we offered them to act together, to call a meeting, for example, and discuss all questions there and even perhaps, to make up a letter on behalf of the whole collective to the government bodies,—surely they will understand us and render us assistance,—none of them took the responsibility, saying that our people are ignorant and the authorities don't approve of such meeting and collective appeals to upper instances,—you're just visitors, and we're to live and work there, so if you're going to undertake something, do it without us. That was the kafkian labyrinth with no outlet. Nevertheless, indignant, but without losing one face, we decided to send one of us to the district centre. We chose Bolot. He met the authorities of the district and discussed with them the question of roads and bus communication. Why, I ask you, comrade so-and—so, don't you work as you are supposed to? Why do you waste your ardour on me, why do you look at me with such hateful eyes? Why, I ask you, do the people from Kysyl-Suu have to get to the centre by lorries covered with tarpaulin? Why do passengers have to suffocate with dust and cram, sitting on each other in the body of the lorry like herrings in tin?

It's a real hell, get me right please, you, who own a car from the state, why must pregnant women and old men must be jolted on inconvenient boards on mountain roads? Moreover, lorry-taxis like this only make one trip a day, to and fro, and if there is some breakage, Kysyl-Suu becomes isolated from the rest of the world for two-three days. You ask me where I am from? I am from Kysyl-Suu, surely, from where else I could have been. Of course, I did not tell him of Jolchuby's dream. Unfortunately, even he shrugged his shoulders, saying that he understood us, but could not assist us in any way and I'd better not interfere in all these affairs.

We had quite a bicker, he even threatened me to go to the procurator. But then he calmed down and uttered: what about the road? The Ministry of Transportation won't permit long distance buses because the road are too bad. I'm sure this can't be true: it is an ordinary mountain road like any other in Kyrghystan. Why isn't there any transport to the centre of the district? The distance is only 50 kilometers. In comparison, the 500 km. tract between Frunze[19] and Kazarman had regular trips. The district authority answered that he did not know, that he acted according to the instructions, the law. And what were we supposed to do, those who didn't want to follow any orders, but only our hearts? To take spades, go and repair the road, to make it ready for transport communication? The next time it was my turn to fly to the capital as a representative, to meet with the Minister of transport communications of the republic. He listened to me attentively, shook his head, agreed with my thoughts, and when I was almost about to believe that he would help us—he diffusely said, that the problem was being attended, he even put down the name

---

[19]   Frunze—now called Bishkek, the capital of Kyrgyz Republic

of the village, but nevertheless, he did not give any promise. Then he received some telephone call and I had to say "good by" to this important person, I was so lucky to meet with. He not only received me, but also talked to me for seven minutes. He might have refused me at all as well.

Also I visited the Ministry of Communication, though nobody told me to do so. I decided to take my own initiative once I happened to travel so far, there I met another important person, though he was not the Minister himself. There I decided to go straight to the heart of the matter at once, though the previous meeting with the Minister damped my ardour a bit. Why is the communication with Kysyl-Suu so bad? Reallly bad. Only yesterday I visited the central telephone office and had to wait for 2 hours until I had been connected with Kysyl-Suu. Indeed, it is easier to get in touch with some point in the Far East had to little white, not mentioning the quality of communication, when we call to our village, the connection was so weak, as though Kysyl-Suu was located somewhere on Mars: a scarcely audible voice reached you as if through a storm, disappearing at all every now and them, while Vladivostok was heard so distinctly that you could distinguish a voice from the next cabin. Is it really impossible to change the cables and wires so that voice of your phone subscriber would not be heard as if from the other world? You are certain to fail to get a right person by phone the next time; either the line is out of order, or a telephone girl is off to drink her tea, or you got misconnected again, or the automate was broken, or a swallow sat on wire. You are hardly to succeed trying to get in touch with Kysyl-Suu, no matter how strong will and endurance you have. What is the use of such communication? To scoff at a man, exhaust him and frustrate his plans and hopes? The Ministry of communication executive sympathised with our situation, and then after a short silence he said rumpling his forehead that it was a burning question in our Republic, that the time would come when all telephone lines would be replaced by modern equipment, that there were instructive and reliable projects on that account. But when would they be put into practice—when? That was the point. Mankind is on the brink of mastering telepathy as universal biological means of communication, and as for us, still having trouble with that outdated rubbish. Oh God! time is pressing, we can not wait till the next Five-Year Plan. We should gather all our strength in order to make a breakthrough toward the future. Ekh, Kysyl-Suu, if you only knew, who was coming at you, if you could only feel like a living person, not like a mass of downtrodden people. Perhaps then you would awake from your age-old slumbers, put yourself into a proper order for a few days and weeks. The people would begin to move, to bustle and their natural pride would begin to seethe, to look for a way out of the situation,— and would find it, surely, settling accounts with "well-wishers" and "wardens", who got used to treat the people as a milk cow, giving everything she has and requiring nothing in return. Most mentioned, big bosses" were really convinced that our people did not even dream of something better, that they even don't eat the black caviar, if someone offered them to eat it, but they themselves a perfect judges of life, with a nice taste and an excellent appetite and know how to make use of people's ignorance and inexperience.

The paradoxes of high improved and obscured societies

That is truth,
in England
all people have looked as polished talents and genius,
even a driver there
or porter, or steward,
or begger, or trader,
or stealer, or priest,
or head of ministry
do not work without great quality and service.
There is, seem, only one stupid man—mister Bean,
who prevailed all brilliant persons given together.

They are all have made themselves
as they want and planned
through successful work
and competition
in various branches and activities
of high improved community,
while the others unlucky
inhabitant of authoritarian countries,
post-soviet states
and Islamic caliphates
as the Iranian regime
that must proud only with Omar Hayam
in last millennium,
have had a very small portion
of really famous and respected men
or just intrinsic professionals.
And their waste majority
looks like as screws in clock's engine,
or as soldiers in training camp of rebuilding empire,
or as religious fanats in Friday namaz
or as new slaves
in collective farm and weapon producing factories.
They have not any chances
for arise to personality
in terms of quality and standards
so usual for British community.

V

Well, let us drop it, suppose we would not give free such tedious
details of our life to the fiancee of Jolchuby, suppose we would take
her to Kysyl-Suu on a hired taxi with pink curtains at the windows.
And what to do next? She had been dreaming of that land for many
years, living at the far end of European Continent, on that foggy
island near the English Channel and there she was coming at last, a

proud daughter of Albion, overcoming all her doubts and fears, ready to go round the world for the sake of her love.

But we did not give in, even when life circumstances, people and social environment were constantly threatening Jolchuby for different reasons. All that only strengthened us in our resolution to carry everything out. We effectively changed the living conditions in the village; we managed, for instance, to replace the roof on the house of Jojchuby's parents, to paint the floor. And the most successful thing we did was to make a fire-place. In the living room there was fitted stove from clay used only on holidays and cold days, so we remade this prehistoric stove into a real English fire-place, very accurately and with a special inspiration, building it with excellent burnt brick, and installing a metallic fender. The parents and brothers and sisters of Jolchuby liked this modification very much.

We were so happy, that the relatives of Jolchuby liked our invention. But there was so much work to do, though we got many helping hands we could not manage. We were to have the yard put in model order, have the summer house restored and repainted, and the most important we wanted to do was to pave the way from the house to the gate, to the tandyr[20], the toilet, the stable. With autumn rains coming the roads would be made impassable by rain, you could not take two steps without sticking into to mud. So, we paved the pathes with stone, there was enough of such material around the ail. But for putting ideal order and guarantee absolute cleanliness, all roads leading from yard to yard, to the school, to the shop had to paved with stone. We should put an end to the mud in the whole ail at the same time or wait with angel-like patience for a miracle to happen. We were not ready to perform such Hercules deed. Where, in which Kyrgyz village do you happen to see a complete net of such roads? We consider paved paths as trifles, though not without envy watch English villages, where all that trifles get more attention, they understand, that roads are an interior circulatory system and its state is the indicator of the physical health of the whole organism. By our

---

[20]   tandyr—stove, oven for baking bread

personal concrete example we showed the whole ail what can be done within a short time, what order was and what profits it had. At first most of our fellow-villagers regarded us as cranks, but as the work went on, seeing that we were not afraid either of summer heat, nor drudgery with clay cement, wood, they changed their opinion, they looked at that all with different eyes and began to envy Jolchubys parents. "God himself sent them such builders, so quickly and coordinated they worked".

But all we had done—are working of the house, the new fence, the paved paths, the summer shower was just a prelude, just a beginning of the great work, because within a short time all we managed to do was just a slight make up to disguise the most visible defects. And after that, when we would have enough time we would rebuild everything to stay for ages.

Yes, we would have to commence everything from the very beginning, to change our mode of life and ourselves. The work doesn't end, work to which the Kyrgyz are least of all used, laborious and tireless work, that brings its fruits not at once, like the labour of a farmer or gardener. Although people around us understood us well, that did not give the aspired results, as everybody was busy with his own work and worries. Beside our, timid" campaign, there were many other campaigns, far more celebrated and official, directed by the highest instances. These were both the gathering of hay for public cattle, and shearing of sheeps, and the hard working during harvest time on the cotton fields, to which the whole ail would be mobilised. All those campaigns were less effective than ours, they did not give you satisfaction. The workers of Kysyl-Suu didn't get anything for the laying in of hay, for the gathering of cotton, for the breeding of common cattle, on the contrary, it was all taken away, as sheep, pastures, territory and water did not belong to you, but to the state, which got used to exploit the labour of the people in order to feed it's numerous bureaucratic apparatus. Anyway, people got used to it— and nothing could be done about it—at least not within a second, instantly, right now.

The plain comparisons
for our shepherds

Then more you will love all English
and deeply obsessed by them,
than more you have been progressive
and ept and fast for gaining success,
and granting by freedom and blessed.

Then more you will love Russian
in temporal staff and condition,
than more you have been temptative
by post-soviet integration and stagnation
and trapped by sovereign democracy
and rule by ambitious and dictators.

Then more you will love Arabic,
then more you have been islamic
with turban on the head
and Koran in the heart
with chronic problem of technology
and prisoning himself, women and others
in oldest concepts and methodologies
from Al Kasim abu Bakr mister Mastodontes.

Then more you will love German
then more been precise and prosperous.
Never forget about it, chaban,
if you want to ride Mersedes, Opel, Bantley
in the company of kind and free persons
blessed by future elegancy.
Not in company of terrorist,
fanats, imperialists and others banditti.
riding the junked autos,

with weapon of mass destruction
and prehistoric instincts and traditions.
That is clear comparisons and bananas
for our dear shepperds, chabanes.

VI

Most of them would agree with our arguments, but they kept saying that everything would be better the next day, in the future, and today the most important is to keep your neck from breaking. Surely, in future everything would go the way it should: successfully arranged mode of life, excellent home, favourite work, high culture, everything good will come in future, and now let's work a little more for the sake of the government and state, a little more patience, please,—as if the death itself is whispering these words, trying to divert us from active life, to use us like marionettes in their hands. Today the death is not an old silent woman in a black cloak, today the death is a respectable man, who kills the best in you by postponing everything till an obscure future, till tomorrow. We must get everything today, and not tomorrow. Tomorrow means never. How could we let Jolchuby, his love, his future down? That was the question.

In one of the most anxious moments for us, we addressed the director of the sovchoz.—Agai[21], is it possible to live the way the Kyzyl-Suu people do, there aren't any conditions: neither a rest home, club, cafe, nor a stadium or a dancing floor? After all they should at least have a public bath-house? How do three thousand people manage without it? And what about a swimming pool, a theatre, beauty salons, chess clubs, museums, different native painters and amateur photographers exhibitions, a zoo—all this they can only dream of. But on the other hand almost every kolchoz in the East Germany has its own zoo, besides there are countless museums. What place can you suggest for culture, happiness and prosperity to flourish? Ha-ha-ha,

---

[21]   agai—(kyrg.) master, teacher, old brather

agai, you are absolutely right—what zoo do we need in Kyzyl-Suu, where we live ourselves like animals in an unfinished safari park, surrounded by the stone wall of these mountains. You just have killed us, agai, and yourself too. Certainly, we fully agree with you. It is too early for us to measure our strength with more developed countries of the world, but we have to escape from this thick swamp. The director seemed to be a simple, with sense of humour, understood us, he said that he had been building a bath-house, but it turned out that the place had been wrong, too close to the river and districts sanitarian attendants hadn't permitted its exploitation, that is it. Well, we always have such problems, we construct and create, but in a clumsy way. What use of a bath-house like this? So, what can one do, the kolchoz director shrugged his shoulders, I have been working here for half a year only, I am still very green here and don't account for faults of the last one. Yes, when you've worked here for two or free years, we told you, we will ask you again. If you are not by that time transferred to some new place, where you are nothing again. Just confess, what a stupid system, when nobody is responsible for anything, just changing the places. Don't be offended: we don't mean you especially, but in general the leadership sent us from the top. To pay for it all are ordinary people, who won't move from their place.

But what are we to do in this situation? What can we rely on and hope for? Why wasn't Jolchuby born in another district, which has deep and firm traditions of sensible, careful and scrupulous business management? For instance in our popular kolchoz "Russia" of the Nookat district, where, judging by everything, all necessary conditions for a normal human life are present: bath-houses, a Culturepalace, a gymnasium, a sportcomlex. That kolchoz differs from Kyzyl-Suu like heaven from earth. Yes, indeed, we weren't lucky, and the genius, damn him, was born in that by God forsaken spot. You ask me who this genius is? And who do you think then, is Jolchuby? If you don't believe me, try to do what he did, only he knows through what obstacles he had to surmount in order to get into contact telepathically blindfold, giving up everything to find his love. And the most pitiful fact was that having accomplished the most difficult part, minor sorrows almost seemed to tackle us. Jolchuby had really left us too far behind. His future love seemed impossible and unreal from our present points of view.

But let's suppose that the devil take this bath-house and the palace of Culture, which aren't likely to appear in the ail. After all Kyzyl-Suu is not all of Kirgizia and the republic doesn't end with this Godforsaken spot. Why can't Jolchuby live in town with his beloved in first instance? In Osh or even in Frunze? We'll be able to help them here: will rent a suitable flat in one of the fashionable aristocratic blocks. It goes without question that they will visit Kyzyl-Suu and in the three years they are in town, having accustomed to each other, there might appear a bath-house in Kyzyl-Suu, cement roads and pavements, maybe a Palace of Culture, a modern station, a winter swimming pool. This will be the happy end, the happy outcome for such a problematic and troublesome love. Never will Jolchuby's Eleanor regret for her youthful decision to take such a risky step, not listening to the advice of bold fat vicars and priests. Even after many-many years of happy life she will become a wise and respectable baibiche[22], grand lady, apah[23], even then her smile will remain as marvellous and charming, as it was the first time, in the dream of that red-haired guy, and never will she—have to dry the tears in her blue eyes after saying goodbye to the gusts and staying alone, never will she whisper to herself those ever womanlike words: "it's all right, only something lacks". And the main thing, your love will become the talk of the town, will turn into a national dastan[24], a romance, a splendid song, which will be sang by many generations, you'll see. So, it's not just love, makhabat[25], but something higher and even greater,—it is really a unique bridge between two very different and very remote people and part of world. I think, this is a honour not only for us standing on this side of mirror, but for England also, isn't it, ladies and gentlemen? Therefore, let us not be limp, the whole world looks

---

22 baibiche—(kyrg.) matrona, grand-lady
23 apah—(kyrg.) mother
24 dastan—lyrical poems
25 makhabat—(kyrg.) love

at us. Jolchuby, what's the matter with you? Don't you now see the light at the end of the tunnel, more than light, the real sun!—soon we are in a wonderful Victorian garden. If you don't mind, when you are mowing to Kyzyl-Suu with your girl, we all will also go there, not for a visit or a holiday, but forever, we'll live next to you, will create our own airville[26], town of the future. We all will live together until we all retire. I will do everything for your happiness, to cheer up Eleanor, don't hold me for a bad guy, actually I can't like blue-eyed ones, but for your sake I will make an exception. And when we are all pensioners, we'll be the most authorised and respectable people in Kyzyl-Suu, we'll teach the youth and at our home they will learn much about the Orient and the West and about the possibility of bringing them together.

So, everything will be all right, Jolchuby, don't you even doubt. The more so as your girl, judging by everything, is a really clever girl, she may now be seeing all and feeling all at heart. You think they have no problems there. Enough problems, even though it's one of the highly developed states of the world? Oh, by the way, Jolchuby, do you happen to know the profession of Eleanor's parents? Miners? That's OK, that means they are ordinary people, understanding ones. I was already worrying: maybe she is a daughter of some peer, lord, House of Commons member or of a multimillionaire capitalist. Just imagine, how difficult it would be for us!—But they are entirely different people, and our Kyzyl-Suu . . . no, I just can't imagine our future living together.—It's all nonsense, buddy, it's nothing more than love delirium,—am I right, fellows? You know, you used to say that your favourite Hardy, was one of the most "Kyrgyz" English novelists, that depict England, his strange characters and their fates, intonation of the narration itself, its hidden, deep lyrics—it all reminds of Kirgiziya very much. I don't know whether it is all right and objective, but frankly speaking all nations look alike. And the difference is in that fact, that one half of them is a little more developed, a little more dexterous and quick, and the other half can't wake up, rolling from

---

[26] airville—the future towns, experimentally creating in some West countries

one side to the other. The main point isn't this, Jolchuby, but be careful with the next: tell strictly your younger sisters and brothers that a fire-place—is, first of all a place for rest, warmth, comfort, intimate thoughts, flaming up late at night, sitting by the cracking fire, sincere conversations. You should nor fry a stick of kebab on a fire like this, even not for joke. A fire-place is a fire-place, it requires respect, you should only sit near with a beloved, spreading legs close to the fire, sipping through a thin straw a cocktail or tasting wine and hold a cream-of the-society conversation. We can fry shashlik or kebab in the yard—following all rules, on the special frying equipment, remembering to sprinkle it with vinegar and dressing with spices, serve it in the living-room for us with pretty lady—and everything will be all right, you see. Oh yeah, Jolchuby, I always wanted to ask you: will your girl lose consciousness, if she for example, is presented a sheep head as the most honoured guest? In general, the kyrgyz cuisine strikes one with its primitivity,—they boil and pile heaps of meat on the eating table, not concerned about greens and all kinds of pickles and seasonings,—it's incredibly conservative like many other kyrgyz things. Serve us with lumps of boiled meat, that's it! Only this is accepted by our aristocracy, and other things are refused as "not kyrgyz". But that's nonsense, don't worry, Bolot. Meat after all is in fact a fundamental ingredient in cookery, and one can understand our people, because this product has been their bread. The English, as highly developed and civilised people, appreciate first of all measure in everything, tact and perfect taste, they bear carelessness, rudeness and bad manners painfully. This can be judged from the way they thoroughly and neatly look, as if they were going to the Wedding Palace every day to be married. So we should be careful not to make a fool of ourselves—get hold of yourself, if, for example, your tie a little loosened and mowed from its place, or the sleeve of your shirt peeped out of you suit half of a sentimeter more then is admitted, or if you, being an audience, forget yourself and sitting at the table like usually sniffed if only once,—you may consider all to be a waste of efforts, even if nobody noticed it, the English are excessively keen-eyed with such things, anecdotes and limericks may then be spread along both banks of the Thames, they would say that there is such a country,

Kirgiziya, people of which are not so bad, if only they wouldn't sniff at table. It would be a shame! God, beware us! In short, let us abstain from excesses, let's cultivate order. The order in everything is called culture: whether it's cuisine, clothes or your job. It's a pity, certainly, that there isn't hot water in Kyzyl-Suu, why dream of the hot water when there isn't even cold water. The water-supply is missing, though there's a wide river, how long will we keep rattling with buckets and cans, carrying the water from the river! We passed all our childhood on donkeys. What to do—these are the conditions? We have to be patient. By the way, Jolchuby, why are there so few girls in the street? Are they so homely? Is that real life—at the fire-place in the kitchen, when does the 20th centure end? Let them, at least once a week, dress, make themselves up and come out to show themselves and to cheer others up. But they are busy working from the morning till the night. Well, allow them at least swim a bit at noon. You shouldn't overload them with so much domestic work, without taking the specific local conditions into account. What if some alien would take a look around here—he would sign deeply, frown his brows and ask: how can you, brothers, exclaim to the whole world about the free woman of the Orient and at the same time let the wrong thing happen? What would you do, answer?—Ah, Bolot, these are all very complicated and difficult questions. They behave this way because they respect their parents, aksakals of the ail. One cannot imagine all the girls and boys, in swimming suits, suddenly before everyone's eyes taking a bath in the transparent waters of the Kyzyl-Suu. It is allowed only to children. You know, they are brought up this way. It's in their blood, nothing can be done about it. On the other hand, it's not too bad, you must understand, actually I have nothing against bathing together, enjoining freedom, the independency of civilized life, but it should be done reasonably, evading possible complications and conflicts, without turning the public opinion against yourself. Why shouldn't we begin to build a private beach, instead of one available to everybody, surrounding it by a two meter high fence in order to keep the sunburnt bodies from keen eyes our aksakal's, until they change their point of view, and coming to the beach they will admit that what we had meant was good, but they didn't understood it the first time, thought we were just bluffing, but would we now please forgive them and allow them to use the beach? Well, the plan reason, but there's no time to waste, you see, Kerim, our generation is not likely to wait for all, I mean we will become the generation of grey-haired aksakals, and it would be probably we, who will be responsible to transgress the border of the beach being looked at by the laughing youth, which, certainly, will consider us to be the main opposes of the new, to be an obstacle in the way of Kyzyl-Suu progress. Or would you like us to bun the youth from the beach? No. You'll see. Everything will be all right when time goes by. Oh yeah, Kerim, as time goes on. What if that time isn't enough, and the people's health doesn't suffice? Health should first place, traditions at the second. Not to swim in such a river like Kyzyl-Suu on a summer day—is quite absurd. For me, Kerim, a woman swimming on a summer day in the river, and if there nothing happens around her—is the music of peace and silence happiness. These aren't my words, nor of some of some western poet, but of our eastern Kaisyn Kuliev. Don't you remember the pity and eternal words of Marx about that, that the relation with the woman is one of the main criteria for the development of mankind in any society. With the relationship between man and women everything starts and finishes: the rising, the decay, the progress and the stagnation. Can you imagine Jolchuby's girl feeling herself uneasily in Kyzyl-Suu? Will she swim alone in the river? Urunissah-eje[27], you are living on the very bank of the river, and you're very modern, educated, and also you're an active member of the female village soviet, relying on your authority, we would like to ask you something exceedingly important matter . . . Why not to set an example to Kyzyl-Suu swim in the river, not giving down about all conversions and customs swim not in a moonlit night with the moon, the way the village girls do, these shy mermaids, but on at midday, to make all Kyzyl-Suu witness this extraordinary action brave challenge to the Orient obscurantism? It's not for us, try to understand us, it's for our people, for their mental and physical emancipation.

---

[27]   eje—sister, miss

We would make a picture of you and try to put it in a paper under the headline. "An emancipated woman of the Orient", "Make way for new traditions" or something like that, and you'll see you'll have the next day followers of likeminded women, you'll be the real hero.—Ha, ha, ha ha! . . . Is it me hero? Ha-ha. Want me to swim in the river? What would my father-in-law think? Do you know what a temper he has? Yes, I agree with you, and want to swim a little, but what you suggest, ha-ha, is impossible, nowadays it's impossible. What we have to do now is to save our men from their drinking problem—problem number one in Kyzyl-Suu. They may then, when their heads are sober, like you, think over our dull and dark existence. If we go so far and plunge to such a detailed conversation, wait a little—have lunch with us.

The shop of political dolls and our idiosyncrasy

Why we have loved England?
Not for the Hide park,
ancient castles
and first class evergreen grasses and pastures,
not for Big Ben, Beatles music and other luxurious,
but for the awkward "puppet theatre"
gamed right on the centre of London,
that horrible and hellish perfomanses
where deformed bodies and figures
of famous politics, majors, prime-ministers
queen members and other up-to-date authorities.
shown as personages of harshly sardonic drama.

That popular and profitable business
in Albion—creating and selling monstrous shapes of theirs
excellencies
on the open exhibition,
so sharply contrasted with our own preferences
and quite other way of arts perfomanses
practising by our narrow minded artists
deformed sculptors, wicked painters,
enslaved writers and other arts dicreators
survived by creating innumerous golden statures
of our "purest" top governors, "idyllic" leaders,
"angel like" thefts, cleptocraties
and others political idolatories
from our autoritarian idiosincrazy.

VIII

At such meetings and conversations, philosophic debates and revelations—sad, blue, funny, amusing—our agitation campaign was going on without basic hopes for immediate success, but nevertheless making a strong impression on Kyzyl-Suu people, inspiring them—this way we've been teaching others, and at the same time we learnt ourselves, began to understand each other and the surrounding world better. Time went by and 20th October 1984 drew near.

Sure, we didn't accomplish a revolution in Kyzyl-Suu, this wasn't even our task. Kyzyl-Suu will certainly be reformed, because everybody wants to live better, fuller, although nobody know where to start. Principally, people were ready, problems which aren't solved in decades, gave an tremendous oppositional power. And, it seemed that just a little crack in the dam could make it crash down the next minute under the enormous power of water, yes, these people were really ready to correct the mistake tomorrow, even though time speeds up more and more, as if it were some missile, taken off to space. How difficult it is to compare with time—try to take hold of the missile taken off. Everything rushes and shakes with dizzy speed, everything changes every minute and there's no time to take a breath, everything is on the run. Even in this remote god-forsaken place. The grey-haired aksakals, the green silly youth, the young people-reformists, like we are—all, without an exception, were driven crazy trying to catch time. Someone tries to arrange a lucky marriage for his son; someone herding sheep in the high mountains dreams of a student life; someone having graduated from the institute and worked a month or two as a livestock specialist or an engineer, says to himself one day "ah, this is not what I need and it's just a waste of efforts and money", and he has to begin from the very beginning; someone governs; someone works in the mines; someone on goldfields; someone on the building the new cascade for a hydro-electric station on the Naryn—in general, the mill of life rotates everything into good order, undoing the rudeness and imperfectness, inherent in life, and every day more and more people find their place in this life, it means that our society becomes more perfect and harmonized in all aspects. Don't worry, everything will be all right, Jolchuby. Look at the things that happen not only from the present, but also from the future, compare your inner problems with those global ones, over which the whole world cracks it's brains, solve them step by step in the world gradual movement to the light, context, and every moment your spirit rushes to heaven, be always close to the earth, as we were all the time, then you . . . never guess your fortune, won't live in vain.

But, as the critical day was drawing near, Jolchuby gradually lost courage. It seemed to us that was going to be all right and though the enormous iceberg of everyday problems that pressed on us, didn't move a millimeter and wasn't even going to, it began to melt and somewhere inside of it a shy spring stream ran. And when the last decisive month came, our telepath became absolutely crazy, he gave up all his (and our) plans and with a power comparable to that with which he created his wonder-bridge, began to destroy it. First of all he to persuade us that a mistake slipped into his calculations, he showed us his schemes and diagrams, a computer account, which nobody understood, assuring us that to make an appointment in a dream is possible, it means to have a sequel of dreams though it's very difficult, but to fix a date yourself asleep with a sleeping person, in the reality—is terrible absurd, no way, the principle of indefiniteness doesn't allow it. Even though someone can see the most wonderful and extraordinary things in a dream, make genius decision; in reality all this is being created by our exhausted nerve system, illusion, no more. But Bolot objected against this mentioning Einstein, Pushkin, Mendeleev, and that the Jolchuby's discovery wasn't so great among them: the periodic systems or the theory of relativity were more difficult to discovery, then to find your love. Then Jolchuby began to cheat, that he had been throwing a bull all that time and had made up that unbelievable story the idea of which had once come to him when dreaming. But we didn't believe him at this time too and told him never to wind us around your little finger.

Namaz for Wests values

I don't know,
weather God speaks on English or not?
But that is exceptionally important
for us
learning as quickly as possible
this exellent tool
for business, global managment,
human rights and honestly governing—
for the sake our salvation, independence and prosperity.

Had better if we were prayed on English,
as our grandfathers turned for God through Arabia,
and late learned to create namaz for Kremlin
and Communizm on Russian.

O great Lord,
who are lived everywhere and nowhere.
Bless us

the same way as did it for US
that have ruled by unknown leaders
and with firmly hand of democrasy
since the end of XVIII centure
whem fathers of american freedom
proclamed independence of states,
as the Germany and Japan after World War II,
conveyed to free sociate
by westerns generals and economists,
as the Singapore
ruling by firm hand of Lee Quan,
gone for freedom,
we are ready live short time
under pressure someone like Pinochet,
if he only know really where to go.

Please, great Lord,
just not to leave us
and our children and grandchildren
under the guide of fundamentalists,
postcommunists, imperialists
and others maniacs of history.

IX

In short, our Jolchuby began to give in. The load, which he had laid on his shoulders, turned out to be backbreaking even for him, a mighty and strong person. This is at live can do with you! Till you win this struggle, you are grey-haired, as thin as a straw, and when you receive what you wanted, it becomes clear, that the first troubles are on their way to you, and that what is behind your back, was just peanuts. Love—is climbing the height, where to stay is as difficult as to climb it. You can change nothing, that is love, even if it is ordinary love, but in Jolchuby's case it is complex, polyform, intercontinental, fantastic mixture of reality and dreams, it goes without saying.

We tried to inform our relatives, to pave the way for that principally new situation, which would arise out of Eleanor arrival. We concealed the most important thing, not saying them who would come.

But it was already difficult to make Jolchuby change his mind, he seemed to believe that he was mistaken from the very beginning, that what he told us was nothing more then delirium, and that he really feared to be known as a madman, which was really the most scaring for him,—"you know how I hate pathology, in whatever form",—these were his old words, the more and more repeated now.

In short, again we weren't lucky—after so much efforts and losses! Life has mixed again all our cards and plans, swept all the chessmen off the chess table with its childish careless hand, saying "patience, patience, my beauty is in enigma and incomprehensibility". Damn it, if the efforts of many years go to hell. And one would be a complete fool to let pass such a brilliant chance to catch the Blue bird. Everything was ready—one more try and the gates of paradise would be open. What are philosophy and people, became so lazy and apathic, that they can't even do what is prepared! Jolchuby, you, no doubt, acted like a real Kyrgyz on the most important moment of your fate. We were sure, that everything was done, was behind, but at the last moment you turned your back and went away, making yourself ashamed. Oh, if such a girl had loved me, I would do everything for her! What, the hell, did she see in you? As for the height, but the physiognomy not nice, happy return and wish, no more and what about the common sense, nation self-respectness—it is absent. Absolutely. How are you, poor Kyzyl-Suu, poor fellows, lucky! Oh! You did wanted to wind us around your little finger. As for me I didn't believe a single word of what you told us. Without saying anything I left on the 18st of October for Moscow, while you acted like a milksop . . . fearing further complications in interesting propositions, when it is possible to wag the tail, addressing to holiness and stableness of the soul calmness. Damn it, your hellish soul calmness among the virginal clear mountains of Kyzyl-Suu!

I spent two nights at the station—I never thought it would be so difficult to settle down in the capital's hotels!—on the third day, on the 20th of October 1984, at 3 o'clock Grinvich time I arrived on the Red Square at the monument to Minin and Pozharsky. She didn't make me wait a single minute, as our beauties, who want to test the strength of the youthful love making their beloved wait at least half an hour. I tell you, Jolchuby, everything even turned out more excellent than you could imagine in your telepathic dreams. Having noticed me, she moved at once in my direction. I stood like a stone excited and worried very much, but nevertheless, I was able to keep myself under control. She asked immediately: "Where is Georgeby? She understood at the first sight that I was your close friend. To tell the truth, I also recognized her at the first sight, when she came up to me out of the crowd, which streamed from the Kremlin, even though I had never saw her in my dreams as you did. What a beautiful creature you contacted and fascinated! Probably Uanessa Redgrave looked like this when she was 20. You know that the Red Square is called so because there is a plenty of beautiful people always there, who come from all over the world to look at the Kremlin, you can meet there many beauties, but even in that wonderful surrounding your love set everyone in the shade. I felt it almost physically myself standing next to her. Do you believe, I have never been envious of someone, but in Moscow I regretted sincerely that I wasn't in your place, sob. At the same moment it occurred even to me to pretend to be Jolchuby, and if Eleanor all of a sudden took me for her lover, chosen telepathically, I would do my best in his place. But it was impossible. She understood everything at once from the first moment. I didn't know what to say to her—she seemed to see through me—started to stammer in a mixture of English and German, in short, lady, we are sorry, but your friend is . . . ill, can't walk, and he sends you his love.

I seemed to say it, anyway I scattered a growing anxiety in her eyes. But to try to deceive Eleanor Rigby, this peri[28], gifted with clairvoyance— was not simply hopeless but a shameful affair. In short I foolishly meshed things up because of you, Jolchuby. By the way, she seems to surpass you

---

[28]   peri—(kyrg. mifical creature) heavenly girl, angel

113

in telepathic gifts: you couldn't decode her real name in your dream, but she decoded yours, and not only your name but the names of your close people and she even knew in general what they are doing and as for your parents she knew as much as any other daughter-in-law wouldn't learn about her mother-in-law having lived with her for decades. She asked me about your parents feelings, whether your elder brother got well. What's the matter with him? Something serious with his throat? You see, I knew about it from her. Imagine, Jolchuby, you were ashamed for your people before her. Isn't it a miracle? To understand to such an extent, to get to know you without meeting you and your country. Moreover she asked me about it all in such a way, as if she were thinking how to help you and your people in the future. Probably, she had learned from her doctors in England because she understood that in the motherland of her lover the medical service is wretched. On the one hand it is understandable, you know, Jolchuby, you were mainly transmitting functions, while she receiving more signals, on the other hand women are more sensitive to those phenomenons, especially such women as Eleanor Rigby, outstanding, strong persons, though their may seem fragile and etheral. Do you ask how she was dressed? Yes, as in your dream—she was all in white: a white autumn jacket, a white dress, white shoes; an ideal sportive figure—what else do you want? Oh, her earrings with precious stones were shattering, her graceful handbag was over her left shoulder. Generally she made herself up to meet you. You humiliated me before her Jolchuby—for yourself, for Kyzyl-Suu, and for everything in this unrealised unmaterialized long story. I started out again to use cunning, already in the sort of your dead hero-telepathy, I began to tell her about those difficulties and problems, which we all make through in order to say after all that it would be better to live apart from each other, Jolchuby, that there was no way out. I tried to assure at last that everything would change for better in future. Yes, I was going to say it, but when I dared to look up I stopped short at once and felt silent . . . Her gentle face became deathly pale, she knew everything, she read everything in my single glance and I understood that telepathy was a more serious thing, then even we— it's adherents could imagine. Judging by the little narrowed and darkened eyes and the hardly noticeable trembling at lips, I understood, that she begged me to keep silent, to say nothing. But she had been waiting for you till the last minute, Jolchuby, didn't lose hoping, thought, you was performing her, that you'd pushed me forward on purpose, hiding behind the strangers in this crowded history plats, she thought, that you were watching her to appear before her finally all of a sudden, she was afraid of being out of your taste at the first moments, when she didn't see you. You know, Jolchuby, in England peoples love each other, as in our country and as the whole world, to come over obstacles and problems for sake of a secret date, and to spoil the date could only an absolute idiot, world champion amongst the fools.

The enigma of love
from first seeing

We have finding each other's
from first glance
and instance.
How that possible?
I don't know—I just feel that.
And believe as you too right now
that we blessed with the appointment
long waited and precious
with such or other way and occasion
in this world or in other
on a street, in past or future
in a dream or fantasy.
Sometimes soul has seen and proved
the things beyond our reaching and understanding
as a short breakthrough of quantum physic
when our fragile body, consciousness and environment,
betrayed us constantly,
excluding wonders dismissed them with sarcasm and irony.

Our hearts, my friend,
do not a guilty, unfolding to us such acute performances,
and astonishing power and creativity.

He able count and prognoses
with great preciseness
what would have been,
traced and scheduled
in the sacred map of riddles and marvels
long before coming time for starborn.
Better for us just submit politely
the true enigma of first love and mystery
even if you don't believe to love from first seeing
just tell me good bye and good lack
my truly one—so unreal and nonexisting.

X

That moment some girl appeared before us, very nice, with fashionable glasses in a golden frame, who turned to Eleanor—and I heard her original name, but you won't know—you don't deserve it. She, that girl, later turned out to be a fourth-year student at the Foreign Languages Institute of Moris Tores in Moscow. It was her practice to be guide and translator for foreigners, killing two birds with one stone. "Are you sure you liked the place?—I heard the fluent English speech.—Why didn't you call me before going out? You've made it good having warned the hotel administrator, or I would have been looking for you about Moscow? Well, come on, let's go to my place, like we planned the other day, otherwise the monitor will hang me for my leaving you alone". Certainly, speaking that way the girl was angry as a joke rather than seriously: it was absolutely clear, that Eleanor completely fascinated her, the way she fascinated me. "Let's go, come on!" the girl called her again, touching her sleeve, not understanding what was wrong with her, she even gazed at me, supposing that minute, that I was such a gay that didn't know when to leave, hanging on at the wrong moments. But, the girl, noticing her fault, softened, smiling at me. "Come with us!,—I heard her turning to me in Russian.—My mother has cooked such a tasty pie, she worries more than I do about her—and quickly the subject to Eleanor again—Do you know her? You probably got acquainted just now?"—but I couldn't absorb anything anymore, the shock and the disappointment of those minutes were to much for me. I felt, anger was boiling in me, Jolchuby, for our unhappy and wild life, for our pile of unsolved problems, which kill every initiative. Eleanor should have been invited by me, not by that girl, it would have been wonderful to head for the Domodedovo airport, in order to leave for our remote mountain country, the country of her lost dreams, by the way. It's late, late, nothing can be done. I might have lost my consciousness for a moment, I opened my eyes, having been terrified by the thought, what if I would really faint here, at the Red Square,—it, would be funny,— and the first that I saw were—the wide open careful eyes of Eleanor, their sky blue, and then felt her hand on my shoulder and heard her voice, coming from some distance—"What's wrong with you, baby? It's not your fault. I am not offended by anyone. Say him that, do you hear me?" Ashamed, I didn't know what to do, but catching courage, I looked her in the face and uttered the words, she first of all wanted to hear. I said "Everything will be all right—I am sure."—"I am sure too"—she smiled in reply, I've never seen the blue eyes of such warmth and as if they were singing. Who knows, Jolchuby, you may be right—and this girl is too beautiful for us? Inevitably, the time to part draw near, one chance in a million was passed forever and irrevocably, and nothing on earth can turn back time, to begin everything again, to try one more time, the raging and consequent struggle for your happiness—and then everything might be different. But no, it was too late, nothing could be done than to start it all over again, in different conditions. She held my shoulders for a second, her marvellous face in the frame of golden hair, her wide blue eyes glittering—how much love was there, Jolchuby!—and kissed me, there, on the square, in front of many people I guess. Then she mowed away from me, smiled, and, raising her right hand to the chin, made a parting gesture, clearly pronouncing the kyrgyz "Jakshy kal"[29]. And I said her "Fare-thee-well".

---

[29] Jakshy kal!—Good bye!

So they left, and I remained alone in the middle of Moscow. Although the guide of Eleanor, realized the seriousness of the situation invited me once again to visit her—I refused, as my game was over that is your game, our common cause. You can imagine now Jolchuby, the full extent of the humiliation and offence you caused your beloved. It wasn't an ordinary date, can't you see! It's all the same to you, you created her yourself and therefore think you can treat her the way you like. Ekh, Jolchuby, Jolchuby! . . . Why did you mistrust your motherland? Does our country differ from England? What's the hell you think about it? You think they sleep with ties? Eat crocodiles in expensive restaurants? What if it is the richest country of West, if everything could be bought and sold there! It only seems to such simple-minded fellows like you, that they have no problems. It's just a brilliant packing, and inside it there's a rotten capitalism, a society affected by an incurable disease. In our country nobody would betray anybody for the sake of money (for the sake of an idea is another question), and there, in the West, it is all right, it has become a "good tradition" since the time of King Lear that children having grown up throw their parents out of the house. Let us take Kyzyl-Suu, for example, which has no idea of civilized life, but come on, try to explain the inhabitants the essence of Shakespeare's tragedy. They simply wouldn't believe it, and would consider it an enormous exaggeration that daughters could leave their father to the mercy of fate. Isn't it? Well, they are not too intelligent, say, not used to bath-houses, but there is so much humanity in them. So, how comes? Those, who take warm bathes every day, live in luxurious apartments forget about humanity, and those, who live in hard conditions all the time, remain so kind and pure? What a paradox! Although they are backward, and non-too clever they under no circumstances would set you on the street, as happened with King Lear, they wouldn't pretend to be busy or urgent problems have to be solve all time for neglect their everyday humanity duties. Our people inherited those qualities from their forefathers, so we should treat them with care. What were you most at all ashamed of? Of your parents, of us? Of Osh town? Of the dissonance of your native tongue? Oh, love is always shy and timid, but not to such degree. Do you think it was easy for Eleanor?

She realized that in her life happened enough to be ashamed of before us, but nevertheless, she flew to Moscow, in order to meet you and consequently to Kyzyl-Suu. And you, instead of going out to meet her with a smile and soothing her worried heart, you locked yourself up inside your house. The one most close to you person in the world was coming, and you, what did you do? How could it happen? When would fate be so kind to your again? Ekh, Jolchubai, Jolchubai! You would be a king if you wouldn't have been such a fool.

The secret of woman's beauty

What has become as the best makeup for woman?
Her youth, health, nature attractiveness
or just how she get looked to mirror, repaired tresses,
how she smiled and turn to glance?
Maybe mystic lied on her way of wearings,
in her fashion and subtle taste

All these things look as extra-precious
But beauty of soul, perfection of deep knowledge and reason
beyond all competitions and comparisons
as a parts of her grace and eternal elegance.

XI

So Jolchuby brought all our efforts to naught, as later one of his distant relatives, Alibek said: "So that's the way it is? Turned whole ail upside down first and then disappeared completely: we saw neither himself, nor his bride!" What more can one say? Just to ask you, will you be ready, if tomorrow such guests from far away will come to see you in your native village. Can you greet them with appropriate dignity? Doesn't it seem to you, that we are growing out of the traditions of hospitality, we are forgetting it now, just when the whole world get to know about us, when in social life the importance of direct contacts between people is increasing? Or maybe, let nobody from abroad ever arrive in our country? and leave us alone with all our inner problems and troubles, then we would quit to pay attention to them. Then there would be no one to compare with and we would consider our life happy and prosperous. Away with the progress of mankind, let's lock ourselves up in our own narrow world, imagining ourselves absolute god of the universe in a nutshell! The most shameful fact is that a lot of people who would agree with this. Like a man becomes savage and degrades without communication with other people, so a nation can't do without communication with other people, exchanging experiences and knowledge if it wishes to avoid depression and degeneration. Evidently, it is true in respect to civilizations, their further development is impossible without communication with other civilizations, and their being in proud loneliness causes degeneration. And as for Earth civilization of the present as the civilization of homo sapiens, then no matter how rapid it has been developing for the last two centuries, nevertheless, in certain stage of evolution multilateral comical negotiations with our close and remote neighbours will become indispensable. These connections wouldn't be a bad thing at present as well, but other higher civilizations prefer to keep off us considering us not developed enough to trust us, so, the point is obvious, the point is that we, as Earth civilization are not ready to receive visitors from another planets. They treat it with due tact and understanding, even if they wanted to enter into relationship with this silver-blue planet.

But our Kyzyl-Suu story with its a cosmical context doesn't end with it. It seems to begin just now, you won't believe us, but Jolchuby, giving up England, gave up his native Kyzyl-Suu as well, and that fire, we caused artificially, wouldn't die out rather, it begins to grow and flare up, fed by from some inner source though now without our participation. Rumours were spreading and truth got mixed up with fantasy, picking up more and more new details, until, at last, the love story of Jolchuby in the light of our failed experiment become known to everybody. Yes, everything came to light in spite of our efforts to conceal and hide away, at last people all the same got to the bottom of the matter.

Yet, it was the hardest blow for our red Verter, us, his friends failed to make dream come true. Whoever we met in the neighbourhood of Kyzyl-Suu would say with indignation: "How you could fail to believe us?" Most of them were ready even to beat us up, but kept themselves under control by some miracle.

It was extremely difficult for us; even the closest friends would look at us with distrust, as if we had performed something awful. But the most unbearable was the scolding of authorities, that is of those people, who were to be blamed for our failure in the first place. "Why didn't you tell us everything in detail from the very beginning? We are very good at receiving guest! We would have built you and your gelin, hee-hee, a double-storey house in Kysyl-Suu, if you liked. Are we your enemies that we should make fun of ourselves with the whole world as witness? You should have asked our advice, but you preferred to act independent. What a negligence and apolitical voluntarism!"

Then in the houses of Kyzyl-Suu appeared fire-places, it was a real epidemic, then they began to build private bath-houses, houses and yards were being repaired, and the villagers themselves began to paying more attention to their appearances. Shepherd, teachers, workers were caught by fever of accuracy without exception, they began to wear thoroughly pressed trousers, polished shoes. Everything and everybody in Kyzyl-Suu became right and proper, took a strict and respectable outlook. If in the beginning, behind those metamorphosis could be seen ignorance, awkwardness, and light-mindedness, like the wish of some of them to have fire-places without which they would be out of or teenager's mass passion for English rock-music, so that even Kyrgyz songs began to be sung the English way,—but gradually, that the roughness smoothened, it became obvious, that imitations and borrowings from English life became more profound and fruitful. The authorities of the sovhoz had to establish fixed working hours with compulsory two days off and vacation. You know, all this constitutional rights were usually neglected; only Russians and Germans could call on these privileges.

There wasn't any control over such ails as Kyzyl-Suu. The inhabitants of Kyzyl-Suu went almost mad on economic and law categories, and higher instances waste their efforts to bring them to reason. Then they got on strike and went back to work only after thorough calculation of their profits and profits of chiefs, they signed no document if they didn't agree with the content. It became more difficult to deceive them, to pull the wool over their eyes, the way stupid methods formerly did, like upward distortions of the quantity of sheep in spring, and in autumn, when that registered non-existing cattle had been imposed from the shepherd's private cattle under the threat of court examination.

Even the most ingenious combinations of ail bureaucracy's "chess genius" just solid they became in accurate and methodical and solid they became in running their private and public business, as if all of them had got a good training in capitalists exploitation, as if they had become tempered in life struggle forever. If earlier any more or less dodgy crook could simply wind them around his little finger, then such tricks didn't succeed, then everything would be given such a publicity.

In short, though Jolchuby didn't meet his beloved, his love made such a great impression on his fellow-villagers, that it radically changed their outlook and put quite a different order in Kyzyl-Suu, which had obviously become related with the remote Darlstown.

Even when we, the main characters and creators of this story gave up, unable to continue the struggle, the people went on, taking the initiative, full of immense creative energy.

Thus we discovered the intrinsic motivational forces of history, produced by and when it takes possession of the masses. Who could have thought, that those simple-minded Kyzyl-Suu fellows, sons of the mountains, would turned out to be so proud and independent, that they would punish us so cruelly, hurt to the bottom of heart for our distrust and betrayal.

We fell into disgrace, but not like that pitiable drinkers or failures, no. People contempted us the way they would as it could contempt their best sons, on whom they set all their hopes and who failed to reward this hopes. You could never escape their justice, its concealed and sullen contempt would be like a weight on your mind, and you're most unlikely to win the favour the people again.

But nevertheless, in such enlightenment and reaction of Kyzyl-Suu's inhabitants there was something, which Bolot called "light at the end of the tunnel". At least, we were following the right way, if we, and especially Jolchuby, would have enough courage and persistence, then without any doubt, we would win respect and esteem of the people, the people, whom we evidently had underestimated, in spite of all Marxist-Leninist philosophy. If it hadn't been for that, we would have overcome all obstacles.

Jolchuby had little fault, one cannot lump the blame on one person, the more so because he completed his work, he hailed a decisive victory in the struggle with infinity, and let descendant psychologists judge and research how he had managed to erect such an amazing bridge between Kyzyl-Suu and Darlstown, Osh and Liverpool, the seventh wonder of the world, which is beyond the power of time, space, of anyone. Till now we couldn't believe in what that simple shepherd's son had done, that we participated in some way in that striking discovery on the verges of reality and fantasy, dream and reality. Certainly, he spoiled the whole picture and his former services by his cowardice in the end, but nevertheless, he exists in reality, he is among us. Nobody believed him in the beginning, it is difficult to believe even now, even we, his closest friends didn't want to believe him, being afraid, perhaps, of that formidable responsibility, which would follow, now we are aware of it, the fact of the miraculous achievement.

Nothing rests us than to seek consolation in this magnificent sunset over the ancient town. There's always an inexpressible and inimitable charm in the twilight over the town of Osh, caused perhaps again by this gigantic mountain, by its optical effects. The sunset is as sad, tender and light as the modulative music of McCartney. The sun sets between the two hills of Sulayman-mountain, and falls into the West, where our befriended Eleanor lives. And in the caressing beams of the setting sun it seems to us that she understood and forgave us, and that the tomorrow of our country, vegetating in cold darkness in many decades will be much better.

P.S. or real underwater current of this story,
fixed by intelligent services and its great and fatal effects for our time

Certainly Kyrgyz Romeo had not any chance for meeting with his best beloved. Even if she came herself to him from England—arrived to Moscow, and stayed right to the pointed place in time in famous Red Squere, under the one historical monument.

By the way Jolchuby was prisoned by KGB for attempt to communication with "enemy agent" from western countries. The secret agents said to Jolchuby that Eleanor Rigby is very danderous agent from Mi-6. But Eleanor Rigby didn't know about it at all. The KGB agents is working very carefully and precisely. And from the other hand they were said to Eleanor Rigby that Jolchuby had another passion in USSR and didn like to meet with her.

She are counted that Golchuby ignored her and returned to England.

After departing Eleanor Rigby from USSR, KGB had set free Jolchuby but firmly warned him against any contacts with Western visitors, how much they are have been attractive and desirable.

But this love was really unusually strong and great, something happened in deep core of our planet, when Eleanor Rigby come to USSR and returned again to England without any result.

After several years from what happened with Jolchuby and Eleanor KGB and USSR also destroyed and Kyrgyzstan gained liberty and opened for broad world.

And many visitors and friends from West came to Kyrgyzstan and also our people, mainly student, starting to go abroad and learned in Western universities.

And while our hero cannot to join with his best beloved, nevertheless

Kyrgyzstan seems forever joined with England.

Yes, as you see, this is a greatest love in history of Mankind which completely transformed our world.

So if you want keep safe your empire never create any obstacles between truly love hearts.

You shall never afraid KGB and other secret services!

Победи КГБ—не будь моржом!

И ты обретешь любовь и будешь пить боржом!

Kick down KGB and be happy!

Cnange forever the modern history and save Eleanor Rigby from his tragic fate in the song of Beatles:

. . . All the lonely people
Where do they all come from?
All the lonely people
Where do they all belong?

"Eleanor Rigby"

So if you truly love your dear one, you certainly find him and no one empire can resist you.

I will say more, if you are truly love you will able not only completely transform this world, as it happened in this story, but also change the tragic fatum and what had been in past time. As you see we are save our dear Eleanor Rigby. She was returned to England after her 'unhappy' meeting with love in Moscow but her life also comletely changed under the strong influence of the greatest love in history.

The evening Bishkek, south park's district of capital

Instead of epilogue

The empires have died,
even such brilliant as Great Britain,
the oldest and greatest cities
have emtied and crushed for dusts condition again
after thousand years,
even stars on the sky have gone
and constellations deformed their shapes
but only love never die and changing
and creating again marvelous worlds and stories.

Ode to John Lennon

This music has really transformed our world.
It stressed greatly the Central Asia (previous part of USSR) also,
in the time of Cold War and Iron Fences,
when our old fathers-communist leaders,
rotten in power and ruling by Soviet empire till the death,
fighting with freedom, capitalism and Beatles also
as with the decadence and poisoning art of dying West,
until USSR itself collapsed down from stupid governance
and violence and supressing of right of man.

By the way for our olders known
that according with an ancient Kyrgyz prophesy
every millennium bring to world the singer,
who might to crumble mountains and great evil empires
just with his stunning powerful songs.
Now we are going to understand
who was been really John Lennon.
Thank forever, bard of millennium,
singer with Irish-Kyrgys root,
the modern Ossian,
Orpheus who saved our world
and presented freedom for prisoned East.
You are deserved the deepest our respect and love for that
in generation to generation
as long as sounds
this unusual music here and everywhere—
Mind games, Stand by me, Imagine,
Girl, Instant karma, Across the Uneverce.

The half awoken cotton village Nooken
in a summer morning, south Kyrgyzstan

The End